C46026472

KT-579-896

SPECIAL MESSAGE TO READERS

THE ULVERSCROFT FOUNDATION
(registered UK charity number 264873)
was established in 1972 to provide funds for research, diagnosis and treatment of eye diseases. Examples of major projects funded by the Ulverscroft Foundation are:-

- The Children's Eye Unit at Moorfields Eye Hospital, London
- The Ulverscroft Children's Eye Unit at Great Ormond Street Hospital for Sick Children
- Funding research into eye diseases and treatment at the Department of Ophthalmology, University of Leicester
- The Ulverscroft Vision Research Group, Institute of Child Health
- Twin operating theatres at the Western Ophthalmic Hospital, London
- The Chair of Ophthalmology at the Royal Australian College of Ophthalmologists

You can help further the work of the Foundation by making a donation or leaving a legacy. Every contribution is gratefully received. If you would like to help support the Foundation or require further information, please contact:

THE ULVERSCROFT FOUNDATION
The Green, Bradgate Road, Anstey
Leicester LE7 7FU, England
Tel: (0116) 236 4325

website: www.foundation.ulverscroft.com

THE FUTURE MRS. WINTER

When Carey Ashmore's friend Jake asks her to pretend to be his fiancée for a few days, she sees it as a chance to enjoy a holiday in the sunshine. What she doesn't reckon on is the brooding but gorgeous Max Winter, a fiery redhead called Rebecca, a drunken aunt who knows all the family secrets, and a deranged ex-boyfriend. Fearing that she's fallen into a Daphne du Maurier novel, Carey begins to wonder who she can trust.

Books by Sally Quilford
in the Linford Romance Library:

THE SECRET OF HELENA'S BAY
BELLA'S VINEYARD
A COLLECTOR OF HEARTS
MY TRUE COMPANION
AN IMITATION OF LOVE
SUNLIT SECRETS
MISTLETOE MYSTERY
OUR DAY WILL COME
BONFIRE MEMORIES
MIDNIGHT TRAIN
TAKE MY BREATH AWAY
THE GHOST OF CHRISTMAS PAST
TRUE LOVE WAYS
ANNA'S RETURN
LOVING PROTECTOR

SALLY QUILFORD

THE FUTURE MRS. WINTER

Complete and Unabridged

LINFORD
Leicester

First published in Great Britain in 2012

First Linford Edition
published 2015

A catalogue record for this book is available from the British Library.

ISBN 978–1–4448–2372–1

Published by
F. A. Thorpe (Publishing)
Anstey, Leicestershire

Set by Words & Graphics Ltd.
Anstey, Leicestershire
Printed and bound in Great Britain by
T. J. International Ltd., Padstow, Cornwall

This book is printed on acid-free paper

1

'What do we make of the fact that we never learn the second Mrs. de Winter's first name?' asked Carey Ashmore. 'Maxim de Winter states that it's lovely and unusual, but not what it is. Why do you think that might be?'

She looked around at a group of blank faces. Not blank in the stupid sense, but blank in the *I'm too terrified to speak up and look like a fool* sense. It was always a problem with a new class, but a few weeks in, the mature students in her latest *Exploring Literature* class were even more reticent than all the others. She'd chosen Daphne Du Maurier's *Rebecca* because it was a favourite even amongst people who had only seen the Hitchcock film. Trying hard to get some sort of response from her students, she pushed aside the uncharitable thought that she might have been better starting with *Thomas the Tank Engine*.

'It says on the internet that Daphne Du Maurier couldn't think of a name,' said Mary. Mary was a no-nonsense woman in her early fifties, with concrete hair and dark red lipstick. She worked in the doctor's surgery next door to the Ad[illegible] Education Centre.

'That's true, Mary,' said Carey, grateful that someone had spoken up at last. 'But what effect does it have on the novel *Rebecca?*'

'Because . . . ' said Sue, swallowing hard and casting a worried glance at Mary. Sue was around Mary's age, with cropped grey hair. She had spent most of her life on the factory floor, until she'd been made redundant the previous year. She had lots of good ideas, but seemed terrified to voice them. 'It makes the second Mrs. de Winter look less important. Everything is about *Rebecca*. The name of the book, and the fact everyone, including the new Mrs. de Winter, is haunted by Rebecca.

Her . . . the heroine . . . not having a first name makes her seem like nobody. In her own right, I mean.'

'Good, Sue. Yes, that's what I was getting at.'

'But,' said Mary, looking daggers at Sue, 'if it's because Du Maurier couldn't think of one, surely that's the only answer we can give.' Carey imagined her talking to patients in similarly dismissive tones, terrorizing them into deciding they didn't need to bother the doctor after all, and that they were sure the knife in their chest would heal up on its own, thank you very much.

'I take your point, Mary,' said Carey, dragging her over-active imagination back to the matter at hand, 'but sometimes, whether an author means it to or not, a novel takes on a life of its own beyond what the writer originally intended. The idea of exploring literature is to think for ourselves a little when we read. Each person will take something different from a novel, and there is no right or wrong answer.'

'So I'm not wrong in saying it was because Du Maurier couldn't think of a name.' Mary appeared to be getting annoyed.

'No, no, you're not wrong at all. But neither is Sue. We could perhaps wonder if Du Maurier couldn't think of a name for her heroine because she too was obsessed with the spirit of Rebecca.'

'It seems to be a waste of time to wonder if the author meant something different,' said Mary, warming to her theme and glaring at Sue. 'It's like all these prequels and sequels. What's the point of them if it's not what the writer wanted?'

Carey bit back a comment about why Mary was in the class in the first place if that was what she thought, even though she wasn't much of a fan of prequels and sequels herself. It wasn't that Mary didn't have a right to voice her opinions, and it could lead to a good debate. It was more the way she dismissed everyone else's thoughts and made them afraid to talk, making further discussion impossible. Carey, trying to understand that deep down Mary was probably as insecure as the others, said, 'Oh look at the time. We've overrun again.' Only by about two seconds, but they'd been the longest two seconds of her life. 'Remember the centre will be closed for the next couple of weeks for refurbishment. It'll give you all chance to get out in the garden to sunbathe. I'll see you all when we return.'

The group filed out, chatting to each other, which was more than Carey had achieved with them that afternoon. Sue seemed to lag behind. 'Can I help you with anything, Sue?'

'I just wanted to say I've enjoyed the class, Carey. I . . . but I won't be back after the break.'

'I'm sorry to hear that. No problems at home, I hope.'

'Well . . . ' Sue looked towards Mary, who was just leaving. 'My husband doesn't really like me doing this.'

It was an excuse Carey had heard many times before. Sometimes it was regrettably true, and in the area where they lived, equal rights in the home had been slow arriving. Sometimes, however, it was just an excuse women used to get out of doing something they didn't want to do. 'I really like the ideas you have, Sue,' she said. 'It shows you're engaging with the text.'

'Yes, but Mary . . . '

They were clearly getting to the root of the problem. 'Mary has very decided ideas, which is great,' said Carey, hiding her own frustration at Mary's intransigence. She wondered how many others in the class were keeping quiet in the face of Mary's domineering personality. There was always one in a group like this, and it was the teacher's job to ensure everyone had their say, but Mary was so overbearing it made it difficult. 'But your ideas are good too, and you should never apologise for them. It's up to you, and I can't force you to come.

Have a think about it over the break. We're reading *The Picture of Dorian Grey* next. I think you'll enjoy that and I'd really like to hear what you have to say about it.'

Sue smiled, looking more relaxed than she had. 'I saw the film years ago. It starred Angela Lansbury and George Sanders. I liked it.'

'Oh, I love that film too! So you have a head start on everyone! I hope you do come back.'

'Thanks, Carey. I'll think about it.' Sue was about to leave but turned back. 'Are you okay, duck? Sorry, I don't mean to be nosey, but we all heard what happened.'

'Don't worry. Not much happens in this town without people finding out. I'm fine, thanks. Shaken but not stirred as they say.'

'Good. He's not worth losing sleep over, duck. A pretty girl like you will soon find someone else.'

'I live in hope!'

Carey said goodbye to Sue and made

her way to the centre office.

'Bad day?' said Jake, on seeing her glum expression. Jake was a good-looking guy of twenty-five. He was one of those terminal bad guys who never really did anything bad, but also managed to get into trouble wherever he went. They'd been friends since university and it was Carey who got Jake a job teaching at the centre when he was fired for the umpteenth time.

'Don't get me started. Why would someone join a class on exploring literature then not bother doing that?'

'Mary?'

'Yeah. How did you guess?'

'I had her in my photography class last year. I think she's done every class at the centre, and taken nothing from any of them.'

'That's a bit sad really, isn't it?' Carey went straight from being irritated by Mary to being overwhelmed with sympathy for her. 'Because she's obviously searching for something.'

'Her imagination. I think she

dropped it down the back of the sofa years ago and can't remember where she put it.'

Carey laughed, but felt guilty for doing so. 'We shouldn't really mock the students. They're all terrified when they step through those doors. On a different subject, are you all ready for the off? The big family wedding?'

'Actually,' said Jake, 'I wanted to talk to you about that. Come on, I'll buy you a coffee in town.'

'I haven't got any money to loan you, Jake.'

'I'm not on the cadge. I . . . I'll tell you when we're out of here. I don't want people listening in.'

An hour later they sat in a coffee bar. 'You want me to do what?' said Carey, almost choking on her decaf latte.

'It's just for the weekend, Carey. It's ideal. You're probably my best friend.' He was stretching the truth a little. They were friends, but not best friends. 'We know each other really well, so we don't have to worry about getting caught out with awkward questions.'

'Yes, but we're about as romantic together as a pair of wet haddocks. No one's going to believe we're engaged. What's the point?'

'My half-brother. Remember I told you about him?'

'Yeah, the American usurper who inherited everything and now holds the purse strings.' She rolled her eyes. It was a story she'd heard more than once whilst at university, and at any other time Jake had too much to drink.

'That's him. He's a monster, Carey. He won't let me at my trust fund till I'm thirty, even though he has the legal right to release it to me.' Carey wondered briefly at the accuracy of that, if the money was indeed tied up till Jake was thirty, but as she'd never had a trust fund, and would never have one, she wasn't sure how they were administered. Jake continued, 'I don't see why I should be broke when he's lording it up in that big house in Cornwall.'

'Maybe he just wants to teach you the value of money, Jake. You know that stuff you're always borrowing off others and not paying back?'

'Do this for me, and I'll be able to pay you back everything I owe. Plus, you'll get a week-long holiday into the bargain. All expenses paid. All we have to do is attend the wedding on Saturday, act a bit lovey-dovey . . . '

'Ew . . . '

'Yeah, you really know how to make a man feel wanted, Carey.'

'You feel the same about me.'

'True. As you say, we're as romantic as a pair of wet haddocks. This is how I know this will work. There'll be no feelings involved. It's not going to be like some chicklit film where we decide we're in love.'

'God forbid.' Carey meant it. There was no unresolved sexual tension between her and Jake. With his sun-bleached blond hair and clean-cut good looks, he was too pretty for her tastes. Plus he was unreliable. She'd lost friends because he'd dated them and then let them down. In fact, if she remembered rightly, he'd taken one of her female friends to another family function with him one weekend and she'd returned vowing never to speak to him again. She had hinted at some other girl that Jake had gone off with on the first night.

'As I was saying,' said Jake, 'we attend the wedding and convince my brother we're settling down. He'll see that I'm being sensible. You are just the sort of girl one takes home to mother, or big brother for that matter. You're wholesome-looking and pretty in a quirky sort of way. You look like Julie Andrews in *The Sound of Music*.' She poked her tongue out at him. 'And when Saturday is over, the week in Cornwall is yours, to do as you please.'

'How are you paying for this? You said you'd got no money.'

'Easy. It's our family hotel and I can stay in any room I want, any time I want. All meals included. Full room service. You won't have to spend a thing.'

'Two rooms, Jake. We're not sharing a room, no matter how much in love we're supposed to be.'

'Okay, two rooms.' Jake stopped and his face spread into a wide grin. 'Hey, that means you're going to do it, doesn't it?'

'I'm completely mad and your plot has more holes than the *Titanic* after it hit the iceberg. But I could do with a holiday, after all that stuff with Dean.'

'Yeah, sorry about that. He's an idiot — you know that, don't you?'

'That's strange, coming from a man who thinks of me as a wet haddock.'

'A really pretty one as haddocks go, though.' She knew Jake well enough to know he was only complimenting her to get his own way. 'Go on, Carey. Say you're really up for it.'

'Okay, but no funny stuff, Jake. I really mean it.'

'Sure. Scout's honour.'

'And the engagement is the only lie

I'm willing to tell. I don't like lying and I don't like hurting people. But I suppose this is nothing like that. It's not like anyone's feelings are involved, is it? It's just about the money you're entitled to anyway.'

'Agreed.'

'I'm not convinced it'll work, mind you, Jake. What if your brother expects us to get married before he releases your trust fund? Have you thought of that?'

Jake's eyes looked furtive, which Carey didn't like at all. 'We'll just have to be really convincing as an engaged couple.'

'Hmm, I'm not sure I like the sound of that.'

* * *

It occurred to Carey more than once during the days leading up to the weekend away that Jake's scheme was less plausible than any chicklit film she'd ever seen, but thinking about her much-needed holiday put all doubts aside.

It wasn't the leaky plot that disturbed her as they drove down to Cornwall early on Friday morning. It was the sudden change of plan.

'You said it was just for your cousin Stephanie's wedding, Jake. One day of pretending, you said, and then I could have the week to myself.'

'I know, I know, and that's all I thought it would be. But big brother has decreed we must all go to dinner tonight.'

'Why didn't you tell him we wouldn't get there in time? He knows you're driving down from Derbyshire, doesn't he?'

'Because I'm trying to get on his good side, of course. Besides, no one argues with Max.'

'Max?' It only occurred to Carey then that she hadn't known Jake's half-brother's name. He'd always been some nameless ogre, or the Orwellian 'Big Brother' whom Jake railed against from time to time. 'Your brother's name is Max Winter?'

'Yeah.'

'And he lives in a big house in Cornwall?'

'Yes, that's right. It's called Manishi.'

'Not Manderlay then?'

'No, why?'

'Never mind. What does Manishi mean?'

'Dunno. It's just what he called his house when he bought it.'

'Despite the years I've known you, I don't really know that much about your family, Jake. Tell me about them. I'll be expected to know some of it, won't I?'

'You know that my dad was American, right? Well, he married Max's mother, Patricia, in the States. She had her own money by all accounts, which is why Max is richer than any of us.' He couldn't keep the bitterness out of his voice. 'Then they divorced and Dad moved to Britain to start up a branch of his company here and met my mother, Diane. That's about it.'

'But there must be more than that. No skeletons in the closet? No uncle who drinks too much at Christmas then gooses the waitress and tells dirty jokes?'

'No, that's Aunt Jane. Not that I've ever seen her goosing waitresses. Waiters perhaps . . . You'll be meeting her tonight. We're not a normal family,' said Jake. 'Dad died when I was young, and Max took over the company, running it from America. Then Mum died and Max came to Britain and took over me. We had a huge row last time we were together. He said I had to straighten up and fly right. He used those actual words. Can you believe it?'

'He sounds scary. Like some overbearing father from a bad movie.'

'He is that and more. I hate him.'

'I never realized that you really did despise him so much. I mean, I know you moan about him all the time, but I moan about my three older brothers. They're a complete pain in the wotsit. But I love them to bits really.'

'Yeah, but you were brought up with yours. Max just turned up when he was twenty-five and I was fifteen and decided he was going to be my dad.'

'That must have been hard, after losing your mum.'

'Like I said, I hate him.' Jake's voice became brittle and harsh. It was a side of him Carey had never seen before. He was usually easy-going, the life and soul of the party. If his brother could make him feel this way, what on earth was the almighty Max Winter going to think of her?

Several hours later, Jake pulled into a long driveway. A mile further on stood Manishi. Carey had been expecting a gothic pile and had a quip about dreaming of Manderlay last night all ready, but the enormous house was in the art deco style of the 1930s with clean white stucco walls. Huge picture windows gave views out over the sea and, Carey noticed, of the driveway. She saw a shadow moving from one of the windows on the lower ground floor.

'It's beautiful, Jake. Like something from the set of *Poirot*.'

'It's alright, I suppose. Of course, Max can afford it . . . '

'Remember you're supposed to be his friend this weekend,' she chided as she got out of the car. In the luxurious surroundings, she became ultra-aware of her black cargo pants and T-shirt, both bought from a supermarket. She only hoped the pretty dress she'd packed to wear at dinner would stand up to Big Brother's scrutiny. That she had to then wear the same dress to the wedding the next day was something she tried not to think about. Whilst carrying her suitcase to the car as they set out, she told herself no one would care. Now, faced with such a magnificent house, she realized that she cared deeply about how she looked. She would be the stain on the carpet and the fly in the ointment in this magnificent place.

'Jake, you made it. Good to see you.'

'Hello, Max. You all right then?'

As she'd been fiddling with her T-shirt, trying to make it look like it cost over fifty pounds, Carey hadn't noticed the man who came out of the house. But once she saw him, she feared she'd never be able to look away.

Whereas Jake was of average height, fair-haired and fair-skinned, Max Winter was very tall and very dark with naturally tanned skin, dark brown hair and dark blue eyes. He wasn't handsome like Jake, at least not in the same clean-cut, rather bland way. He looked like a man who'd lived his life on a ranch somewhere in America, riding horses, rounding up cattle, sleeping out under the stars. She let her imagination wander until she'd pretty much turned him into Gregory Peck in *The Big Country*. His features were rugged and supremely masculine. She looked hard for some similarity in the brothers' appearance, but there was nothing to suggest they were even from the same branch of the human race, let alone the same family.

'And this is — ?' Max was saying. He smiled, showing even white teeth, but the smile didn't reach his eyes, which were probing so deeply that Carey thought for a moment she stood in front of one of the new airport scanners that showed everything. Not that his look was lascivious; more wary and suspicious. As if he already suspected her of committing some crime. It would be a mistake to lie to him, she could see that now, but it was too late. Jake was already doing it.

'Max, I'd like you to meet the future Mrs. Winter.'

'Carey,' she said, bristling at Jake's introduction. She held out her hand and smiled so widely her face hurt. She was immediately overwhelmed by the warmth and pressure of Max's hand enveloping hers. She could feel herself being subsumed by the sheer force of his looks and personality. Yes, it would be easy to be dominated by this man, and might even be quite enjoyable in a way she recognized as innately primal — he was the modern equivalent of the hunter-gatherer — but she wasn't going to allow that to happen. 'My name is Carey Ashmore. I always think it's important to have a first name by which people can address you, don't you?'

2

The inside of the house was just as beautiful as outside. Despite the art deco architecture, the inside wasn't as square and symmetrical. The lounge had been furnished very comfortably with plush white leather sofas, tasteful coffee tables and soft furnishings. The enormous room was at the far side of the house, with a large picture window looking out to the back over the cliffs and the sea, and another window at the other end looking out over the driveway. She supposed that was where Max had been standing when they arrived and that it was his shadow she'd seen as they approached. The thought made her tingle slightly, but not in an unpleasant way.

'The house is beautiful,' said Carey, feeling she had to fill the silence that had persisted between the brothers since Max invited them into the house. 'I asked Jake what Manishi meant, but he didn't know.'

'It's a Sanskrit word,' said Max, seeming to soften slightly at the compliment to his home. 'It means 'desire of the heart'. That's what I felt when I first drove up here and saw it. It needed a lot of work, but it's been a labour of love. Please, sit down.'

'I'm not surprised you fell in love with it,' said Carey. She sat down on a sofa and was almost swallowed up by it. Feeling a bit silly, she hoisted herself to the edge of the cushion. This was a good way to impress Jake's brother. Letting the sofa eat her whole. She idly wondered how many other visitors were still trapped in its depths and got so lost in the fantasy that she didn't realize Max was speaking.

'I wish Jake had told me about your engagement,' he said, his eyes moving from Carey to Jake then back again. 'It's come as a bit of a shock, so maybe the welcome wasn't as warm as it could have been. I apologise for that, Carey.'

'That's Jake, unpredictable as always,' said Carey, smiling tightly. This was excruciating. Her brothers had their fallouts, and often vied with each other for attention, but whenever they were together there was always an undercurrent of warmth. If one of them needed help, the other brothers were there for them, and also for their little sister. The temperature in Max Winter's lovely lounge was decidedly arctic.

'Strange,' said Max, looking at his brother. 'I usually find him very predictable.' His face broke into a smile, and a rather gorgeous one at that, as if to show he was joking. Carey sensed something beneath the quip. Some edge behind the words. Well, she supposed, if Jake didn't like Max very much, it wasn't unlikely that Max didn't like Jake either. It wasn't her problem, thankfully. 'Dinner will be in an hour. I suppose you two want to freshen up after your long journey. From Derbyshire, wasn't it?'

'We ought to check into the hotel,' said Carey, looking at Jake. He wasn't paying much attention. He sat on the opposite sofa, looking at Max with a sulky expression on his face. He reminded Carey of a fourteen-year-old who'd been given detention. If he wanted to impress his brother, he wasn't trying very hard. Carey began to think that the job of impressing Max fell entirely on her shoulders.

'There's no need for that,' said Max. 'There are plenty of rooms here. I'll have the housekeeper make one up for you.'

One? Carey looked at Jake with alarmed eyes, but he was smiling up at his brother, like the cat that got the fresh fish off the counter. Why didn't he say something about the hotel? 'We've already booked, haven't we, Jake?' she asked pointedly.

'No,' said Jake. 'There was no need with it being the family hotel. It'll be easier to stay here. Thanks, Max.'

'But . . . ' Carey looked from one

brother to another. How on earth was she going to insist on a room of her own? She hadn't planned on sharing with Jake, and quite honestly didn't want to. She had to get Jake alone and insist that he ask Max for another room. She was just about to suggest a moment alone with him when a woman entered the lounge.

To say she was breathtaking was an understatement. Tall and willowy, with a model-girl figure, the woman had long, sleek red hair and was expertly made up. She wore jodhpurs and a polo shirt, but still looked as if she'd stepped out of the covers of a magazine.

'Ah, there you are, Rebecca,' said Max. Rebecca! Of course she was called Rebecca. She couldn't be anyone else. 'Jake has turned up with a surprise.' Once again Carey heard that edge in his voice, but she was too shocked at the new arrival to give it much thought.

'Yes,' said Jake, suddenly deciding to change sofas. He plonked himself down next to Carey, and as he did so the sofa almost swallowed her again. She took it as a metaphor for the way she was feeling. 'This is my fiancée. The future Mrs. Winter.'

Carey was just about to open her mouth, but Max got there first. 'Her name is Carey,' he said. 'She's very keen that we remember it. Carey, this is Rebecca. An old family friend.'

Once she'd picked her jaw up off the floor and righted herself on the sofa, Carey stood up and held out her hand. 'Nice to meet you,' she said. 'I suppose we'll meet Mrs. Danvers next.' Max, Jake and Rebecca looked askance at her.

Rebecca glanced at Carey's hand before holding it right at the end of her fingers. Carey had never known such a half-hearted handshake. 'Nice to meet you, Carla. I think I've heard Jake mention you.' She turned to Jake. 'I had no idea you'd got engaged, darling.'

'It's Carey . . . ' she started to say, but Rebecca had turned her attention to Max.

'Thank you for letting me ride your horses, darling,' she said, her fingers gently stroking his shoulder in a proprietary manner. She turned back. 'Do you ride, Charlotte?'

'No, not as Carla, Charlotte or Carey.' She was aware of Max's lips twitching at the corners. 'I was nearly thrown off a horse at a carnival once and . . .'

'Well I must be going,' Rebecca interrupted before Carey could finish her story.

'You're welcome to stay for dinner,' said Max.

It was Rebecca's turn to assume the look of a Cheshire Cat, and it turned out she was even fitter for the task than Jake. 'That would be wonderful. Do you still have that dress here that I wore to the opera the other week? I had to stay over because of the storm,' she said by way of an explanation no one had asked for.

'I'll ask the housekeeper.' Max left the room. Carey sensed he was angry about something. She couldn't imagine why he'd be upset about people knowing Rebecca kept her clothes there if she was his girlfriend and often stayed the night. Rebecca certainly looked as if she should be Max's girlfriend. She was the sort of woman that a man with his looks should have on his arm.

'We'd better go and get dressed, sweetie,' said Jake, standing up. It took Carey a moment to realize he was speaking to her, and not only that, but he had put his arm around her and stroked her shoulder in the same proprietary way that Rebecca had used with Max. She instinctively wanted to nudge him away, but remembered in time they were supposed to be engaged.

'Yes, good idea. We need to talk.'

'I can think of better things to be doing,' said Jake.

Before a blushing Carey could respond, he was halfway out of the room. She grinned awkwardly at Rebecca before following him.

'What are you up to, Jake?' Carey

asked when they were alone. 'I warned you, no funny stuff.' She stood in the middle of the bedroom with her hands on her hips. It was a gorgeous room. In the centre was a four-poster bed with a white silk duvet. Yet another big window looked out over the sea. Next to the window stood an overstuffed white armchair and a circular bookcase on top of which was a Tiffany lamp. Whoever designed the room had given a lot of thought to comfort. Carey would quite enjoy sitting in that armchair reading, occasionally glancing out to sea, getting lost in her imagination. She had to admit Manishi was nicer than a hotel. More homely, despite the opulence. If only she had the bedroom to herself.

'There won't be any funny stuff. But I could hardly tell Max that we weren't sharing a room.'

'Why not?' Carey didn't really have to ask. It was a rare couple in this day and age who weren't sharing a room, especially if they were engaged.

'Do you really need an answer to that?'

'You could have insisted we stay at the hotel.'

'Carey, are you helping me or not? I'm trying to keep on Max's good side. If I'd turned down his invitation, he'd have been offended.'

'You weren't doing much to get on his good side when we arrived, Jake,' said Carey. 'You were practically sullen.'

'It's hard sometimes when he's such a wanker.'

'He seems okay.'

'That's because you don't know him.'

'Well he hasn't got horns, which was somehow what I expected from the way you described him. He seems civil enough. It was nice of him to offer to let us stay here.'

'That's just so he can keep an eye on me,' said Jake.

Carey didn't believe that fit with Jake's satisfied expression when Max made the invitation, but couldn't understand why. She only sensed that there was more going on between Jake and Max than she would ever understand. 'Anyway, we're getting off the point. You're not staying in here.'

'Where am I supposed to sleep?'

'You can sleep on the sofa as far as I'm concerned! But you certainly won't be sleeping with me.'

There was a discreet cough, and it was at that moment Carey realized the bedroom door wasn't shut. Max stood in the hallway, looking in at them. He'd changed into a casual suit with an open-necked white shirt. She wondered how much he'd heard. 'I hate to break up a lover's tiff, but dinner will be served in a quarter of an hour.' He turned to walk away, but then came back, his eyes twinkling with amusement. 'Jake? There's an empty bedroom next door. It's all yours if Carey doesn't forgive you by bed-time.'

Ten minutes later, with Jake safely distributed to the next room, Carey stood in front of the full-length mirror, not exactly satisfied with her appearance. When she'd bought the floral halter-neck maxi-dress from a chain store, she'd been madly in love with it. But in these luxurious surroundings it looked cheap. Not only that, but it was supposed to be for the wedding, which meant she would have to wear it again the next day. If Jake hadn't sprung their early departure on her she might have had time to throw something else into her suitcase, but he barely gave her time to think. She suspected he'd planned that they'd stay at Max's all along. She just had to find out why.

She pulled at her cropped dark hair, trying as if by magic to make it waist-length and auburn. Apart from her small pointed chin, her face was too rounded to look sophisticated, like Rebecca's. Despite being twenty-five, Carey was often mistaken for an eighteen-year-old. She doubted Rebecca had looked eighteen when she was eighteen. She'd probably been born an elegant and sexy twenty-eight-year-old.

Adjusting her dress so that the neckline wasn't quite so low — something she hadn't noticed when she tried it on in the shop — Carey told herself that it didn't matter. No one would care what she looked like. Why was she getting so hung up on Rebecca anyway? The woman was nothing to her.

Nevertheless she kept seeing the way Rebecca stroked Max's shoulder. But that was fine. They were consenting adults. As long as they didn't do anything to frighten the horses, as Carey's mum was wont to say. Thinking of Rebecca in her riding gear, Carey giggled, showing a dimple on one cheek. She had no idea, as she walked away from the mirror, how very pretty she was when she smiled.

She was a bit disconcerted to find that the lounge was full of people, and all of them were as beautiful as Rebecca, Max and Jake. Apart from one old lady, sitting in a chair near the fire.

She was rather plump and had a matronly air. Max and Rebecca stood talking in a corner. The redhead was looking up at him with adoring eyes. Max looked stern, but judging by Rebecca's smile, she wasn't taking in anything he said. Carey heard him saying, 'I mean it, Rebecca . . . ' The rest of the conversation was drowned out by other people chatting.

Everyone in the room, who had clearly been told the good news, turned to look at Carey as she entered. She feared that they found her wanting. There was none of the joy an engaged couple usually received. She got the distinct impression that they'd switched channels looking for something better, only to find a re-run of a programme they'd never liked in the first place. Where that thought came from, she didn't know.

'I can see, darling,' said Jake, rushing forward and putting his arm around her shoulder, 'that I'm going to have to take you shopping for some new clothes.'

'I'm quite capable of buying my own clothes,' said Carey, caught off guard. 'And I like this dress.' It wasn't strictly true anymore, but her pride was at stake. She didn't want the roomful of people to think Jake kept her in clothing. Added to which, there had been an insult in his words. An inference that the dress she wore wasn't good enough. Even though she felt that way, she was offended by having it put into words by someone else. It made her edgy and uncomfortable.

'I like it too, Carey,' said Max, stepping forward. Carey searched his face for signs of him mocking her, but he seemed to be speaking with sincerity. 'It's very pretty. Would you like a glass of champagne? We're just getting ready to toast your engagement. That's if you and Jake haven't already split up.' His mouth twitched at the corners. Yes, she thought, he was mocking her. He knew the truth, she was sure of it. Any minute now he'd say something and she'd be exposed as the fraud she was.

'Never,' said Jake. To Carey's horror he pulled her to him and kissed her full on the lips. 'We're for keeps, aren't we, darling?'

'Er . . . yes, of course,' she said, fighting a compulsion to wipe her mouth. She knew that if it was a novel, the kiss would have convinced her they were really in love. It had the opposite effect. She could only suppose that heroes in novels were better kissers than Jake. 'But let's not embarrass people by canoodling in public, darling,' she added, through gritted teeth.

'No, let's not,' said Max in icy tones. 'Aunt Jane will blush.' He briefly introduced her to the other guests. Because of her nerves, their names passed her by completely. 'Finally,' said Max, 'let me introduce you to Aunt Jane.'

She was led to the elderly lady by the fire. 'How do you do?' Carey held out her hand and found it clasped in a firm, strong handshake.

'Jake's latest, hey? Well, I daresay you'll last longer than the others. You're a pretty little thing. Come and sit down and tell me all about yourself.'

'I'm afraid that will have to wait, Aunt Jane,' said Max. 'We need to go in to dinner.'

'Well make sure I'm sitting next to Carla.'

'Her name is Carey, Aunt Jane,' said Max.

'Is it? I thought Rebecca said it was Carla. Or was it Charlotte?'

'I get the impression any name beginning with C does for me here,' said Carey, not sounding as humorous as she'd intended.

'And yet you were adamant that it was Carey when we were introduced.' Max grinned, before holding out his hand to help Aunt Jane out of her chair. 'And I don't think we can really argue with you.'

Carey followed them, mentally kicking herself for making such a fuss about her name when Jake introduced her to his brother. He must think her a complete idiot.

At dinner she sat next to Aunt Jane, who was quite helpful in pointing everyone out, giving Carey a clearer idea of who they all were.

'That young couple there are Stephanie and Tristan. They're the ones getting married tomorrow. Stephanie is Jake's cousin on his mother's side. Max is hosting their wedding reception at the hotel. Paying for it all too. Rebecca Wareham is the daughter of an old family friend, and Tristan is her brother. Wareham is her married name. She was formerly Rebecca Pilkington-Smythe. She does look good in the saddle. She could have gone to the Olympics if she hadn't eloped with Ralph Wareham. Her father owns the racehorses, you know. The ones who always win the Grand National.' Carey didn't know, but she didn't want to stop Aunt Jane's flow. 'The two older couples are Stephanie and Tristan's parents. They don't normally speak. Only the happy couple has brought them together.' Aunt

Jane paused, as if she might say more, but decided against it. 'And the three girls giggling at the end are Stephanie's bridesmaids. Two are her sisters and one is Tristan and Rebecca's youngest sister.'

'So how are you all related to Max and Jake?' asked Carey.

'None of us are related to Max,' said Aunt Jane. 'We're all Jake's family on his mother's side. I was aunt to Jake's mother, Diane. But Max looks after us, just as his father did.'

'Looks after you?'

'Financially.'

'Oh . . . ' Carey felt a little embarrassed on their behalf. She wasn't so sure she'd want people knowing that.

'Yes, his father was always very generous with us, and when he died he left a will insisting that Max keep up the good work.'

'I see.'

'Isn't that right, Max?' Aunt Jane said, looking to the man at the head of the table. Rebecca sat on his right, leaning across with her hand on his arm. She'd changed into an emerald-green gown which picked up the colour of her eyes. 'You pay all our bills, dear?'

'Apparently,' said Max.

'And you're paying for this wedding.'

Carey looked down at her soup, wondering if it would be too difficult to slide under the table.

'Aunt Jane,' said Stephanie, 'you don't have to make it sound as if we're mercenary. Tristan is working off the cost of the wedding in Max's firm.'

'And getting a fair wage,' said Max in quiet tones.

'Yes, but another firm would pay Tristan much more. This is something we wanted to discuss with you, Max.'

'No they wouldn't,' cut in Aunt Jane. 'Tristan's not a very good architect. He's lucky to be trained by Max. Oh don't all look so annoyed at me. I admit what no one else does. We're a bunch of scroungers, living off a man who owes us nothing.'

'You could always stop if it bothers

you,' said Stephanie's mother, whose name Carey had forgotten.

'It doesn't bother me because I genuinely like Max. I don't sit here pretending to.'

'So . . . ' said Carey, seeing Max's face darken. She glanced across at Jake, who seemed to be enjoying his brother's discomfort immensely. 'What do you do for a living, Stephanie?'

'I work in a retail outlet,' said Stephanie. She was a stunning blonde with a thick coating of foundation and fake eyelashes. 'But that will all end when I'm married. Tristan doesn't believe a wife should work.'

'Don't you want to keep your career?'

'Why?'

'I . . . well it's just that most women do nowadays. Not that there's anything wrong with being a housewife.'

'No, there isn't,' said Stephanie. 'I shall make a wonderful housewife.'

'Jake tells us that you teach chavs to read,' said Rebecca.

'I teach key skills English and maths

along with literature appreciation classes at an adult education centre. The same place where Jake teaches photography.'

'Yes, he was telling me,' said Tristan, a stocky fair-haired man of about thirty. 'It's one of those grim places in the middle of a council estate, isn't it?'

'Oh, how dreadful,' said Stephanie. 'I don't know how you bear it, Jake. All those chavs. People who sit on their bums all day doing nothing. It's hardly worth bothering. None of them want work.'

'That's not true,' said Carey, starting to feel hot under the collar. 'Many people are unable to work, either because they're ill or they lack the skills or confidence to get a job. Most have been let down by the school system. I think what we do, in teaching people to read and write, is important. And when people properly learn to read literature, to understand the motives of the characters, it helps them to understand their own lives and the world around them better.

Education is power and . . . and . . . ' Carey stopped when she saw all faces pointed in her direction. She was aware of the deep blush that started at her neck and moved all the way to the top of her head. 'I'll get off my soapbox now.'

'Looks like you've got yourself a little socialist, Jake,' said Rebecca, smirking.

'God help me,' said Jake. Carey wanted to throw her soup over him. How could he sit there and not defend the work they did?

'It sounds as if you really like your job, Carey,' said Max. He was looking at her in a way she couldn't fathom. Did he approve of her? Or did he despise her? And why should it matter so much to her either way?

'I love it. Most of the time. I can't pretend it isn't a challenge some days, but no more for me than for the students who do the real work. I thought Jake felt that way too.'

'Love it? Don't be daft, Carey,' said Jake. 'It's just a way of picking up a wage until something better comes along.'

It was no real surprise to Carey that Jake felt that way, but she would have hoped he'd care a bit more about their students than to have them dismissed as useless chavs.

'For you maybe. Not for me.'

'Are you two going to be bickering all weekend?' asked Rebecca. 'Max has already told me how you've relegated Jake to the spare room. Perhaps you'd prefer it if he slept out with the horses.'

'Only if you've no pigs,' said Carey. She smiled sweetly, to hide her fury at Max discussing her private business. Except it wasn't really her private business, as she and Jake weren't a real couple. But still, Max didn't have to run to his girlfriend and tell her everything. Surprisingly, her comment made everyone laugh and the awkward moment passed by.

'So how did you and Jake meet?' asked Rebecca.

'We met at university, didn't we, Jake?'

'Yes, that's right. Then we lost track of each other for a few years, and last year I went to work at the centre and there she was. Looking as pretty as ever.'

'So you got together then?' asked Max.

'No, not then. Carey was seeing someone else.'

'Hang on,' said Tristan. 'So is this that Carey? The one from uni who you used to say was just one of the boys? Weren't you going out with someone else till a few months ago, Carey?'

'Yes, that's right.' Carey didn't like the way things were going.

'And now you're engaged to Jake.'

'Yes.'

'So the one you were going out with . . . was that the guy who . . . ?'

'I don't like to talk about it,' she said quickly, feeling an all too familiar prickle at the back of her eyes. 'In fact, I'd rather not at all, if you don't mind.' She was surprised Jake had even mentioned it to his family. He'd only just started working at the centre, and he and Dean had never even met.

'So,' said Rebecca, 'Jake is your rebound guy.'

'It's not like that.'

'I mended her broken heart,' said Jake. 'She was a wreck when I found her but I put her back together.'

'I was not a wreck!' Carey looked around at the sea of surprised faces. 'I mean . . . it was a bad time for me, yes, but I wasn't a wreck.'

'And Jake was there for you. How sweet,' said Rebecca.

Carey was tempted to tell her that Jake hadn't been there for her at all, and that whilst they were supposed to be friends when all the problems with Dean were going on, Jake was conspicuous by his absence. But that was hardly the stuff of romance.

'What did this other guy do to make you break up with him?' asked Stephanie.

'Maybe,' said Max, 'that's no one's business but Carey's.'

3

Carey stood at the lounge window, taking deep breaths. What a dreadful evening. She'd messed up everything, and it was clear that Jake was none too pleased with her. She half-hoped he'd send her home, and then she'd be free from her promise and from this house which, despite its beauty, was feeling more oppressive to her by the minute. The air crackled with tension, and she wasn't sure if that was on account of her own feelings or because she'd walked into a situation of which she had no understanding.

'Could you try and look a little bit in love with me?' Jake had hissed when they'd all walked back to the lounge to drink their coffee.

'I'm sorry,' she hissed back, 'but no one told me I was supposed to do two performances, and in front of a judge, jury and executioners.'

Once back in the lounge she'd gone to the window, feeling like Billy-no-mates whilst everyone else chatted about family history and friends of whom she'd never heard. She didn't notice Max until she heard his deep, low tones in her ear.

'I'm sorry if you found the questions a bit intrusive.'

She tried to smile. 'Normally when people ask a couple how they met, the questioners feign interest while they talk about how they met over the photocopier, or on the bus, then start yawning when the couple get to the bit about their first date. I feel like I'm in an episode of *CSI*. Do you need fingerprints and DNA too? Perhaps my alibi for the night of whenever?' She knew she was exaggerating. It hadn't been that bad, but they'd touched a raw nerve and forced her to deal with memories she wasn't ready to air yet.

'You can't blame us for being interested. It was a surprise that Jake turned up with you today. I knew he was bringing a girlfriend, but not a future wife.'

'Interest is perfectly natural, but . . . sorry. I'm being rude.'

'No, you're being honest. It was the stuff about your ex, wasn't it? I guess you had a bad time.'

'I really don't want to talk about it, Max.'

'If you ever do, I'm happy to listen.'

His kindness seemed worse than the others' suspicion. It wasn't what she'd expected of him, having listened to Jake's complaints about his brother for so long. Max was rather autocratic-looking, and he disturbed her in ways she was not willing to admit. But from what Aunt Jane had said, he kept a family that wasn't even his, because of a promise made to his father. Perhaps he thrived on the power trip, but it was just as possible he was an honourable man who cared about what his late father wanted.

Paranoia, and not a little guilt about

deceiving him, convinced her that he only wanted to delve into her life so he could find out what the deal was with her and Jake. She replied, 'Thank you, but it's in the past now and I'd like it to stay there.'

'I understand.'

She was tempted to ask him exactly how he could understand what she was feeling, but she was aware she'd been very chippy all evening due to her nerves. If she carried on they really would doubt that Jake would want to become engaged to someone like her. Even though she had no intentions of marrying Jake, part of her wanted Max to approve of her.

It was a blessed relief when people started to say good night. It gave Carey the excuse to go to bed early, citing the long journey from Derbyshire. Yet when she got to her bedroom, she found she couldn't sleep. Her instinct was to pack her bags and leave as soon as possible. Her promise to Jake prevented it. He might behave like an idiot but she wasn't about to be the one to let him down. What a pity he'd broken his promise about putting her in a hotel for a week.

That one day had brought home to her how little time she'd really spent with him, and that was usually in social situations with others. She was beginning to wonder if she really knew him at all. There was something strange going on that she was sure had nothing to do with his trust fund. Not only did his family seem to her to be a rather brittle bunch, but there was a definite undercurrent in the house. Things that weren't being said, not even by outspoken Aunt Jane. She supposed all families had their secrets, and the Winter family would be no different.

Sighing, she put her edginess down to her fatigue. It had been a long day. Not only that, but lies weren't Carey's forte, so to be telling such a big one caused her more stress than she'd ever imagined. It didn't help that one lie led to another, then another, despite her insistence to Jake that she would only tell the one.

She chose a book from the bookcase and sat on the chair next to the window. But instead of reading, she looked out to the sea. There wasn't much of a view at that time of night, but there was enough of the moon to see the horizon. The terrace behind the house had pretty lights going all the way to the cliff edge, where a solid wooden balustrade prevented accidents. The Cornish coastline was breathtaking at any time of the day or night, and she could understand why it inspired writers like Daphne Du Maurier. She was tempted to go down and stand at the balustrade, thinking that the fresh air might help calm her nerves, but as a guest in a strange house, she didn't think she should go wandering about without permission.

She turned out the light, ready to get into bed. It made the scene outside clearer. As she stood up, she saw someone walking along the terrace towards the balustrade. When he stopped there and turned slightly, she saw that it was Jake. He was looking back at the house as if waiting for someone. Curious, Carey watched him. Sure enough, less than five minutes later another person joined him. It was Rebecca. They fell into each other's arms, kissing passionately, and then, huddled together and talking earnestly, they walked along the edge of the cliff and disappeared out of sight.

'Oh my God,' Carey murmured. Jake was having an affair with Max's girlfriend? She felt her cheeks starting to burn again, as if she were somehow complicit in the deceit. Still looking out of the window, as if like a movie another scene would begin, Carey saw another figure leave the house and stand somewhere along the path, looking around. When he turned, she could see it was Max. To her consternation, he looked right up at her bedroom window, then down towards the cliff path with his arms folded and his face, as much as she could see by the garden lights, set in a deep frown.

She stepped back into the shadows, wondering if he'd seen her. If he had, then she ought to say something to him. But what? However outrageous Jake's behaviour, it was none of her business. She had inadvertently discovered a secret that might tear the brothers apart if the truth were known. She wondered if Max had seen them going off together, and that was why he was outside. But why had he looked up at her bedroom? Was he perhaps hoping to see Jake with her?

She got into bed and pulled the duvet over her head, determined not to get involved. She wondered if the best thing would be for her to go home first thing in the morning. She'd promised Jake she'd go to the wedding with him, but she didn't want to be a party to him deceiving his brother. Only then did it occur to her that the real reason she was there was to act as a cover for the affair. Though why the false engagement she didn't know. She could just as easily be a casual girlfriend. It didn't make much sense.

She vowed, as she settled down to sleep, to talk to Jake privately and tell him what she knew. Then she'd tell him all bets were off.

Only, Jake wasn't there when she got up the next morning.

'He said he had to go into town for something,' said Max over breakfast. Carey, Max and Aunt Jane were the only ones there. Everyone else had gone back into Newquay the night before to stay at the family hotel, where the wedding was being held.

'Oh, I wish he'd said. I could have done with a lift,' said Carey. Jake could have taken her to the station so she could get a train home.

'I can give you a lift. I need to go in for a few things. What did you need?'

'Erm . . . a dress for the wedding. I wasn't expecting to need much.' Carey picked at her cereal with her spoon, hating the way one lie led to another.

'But I only brought the one dress and . . . '

'Yes, you could do with something better,' said Aunt Jane, oblivious to any offence she might have caused. Somehow it made her seem less offensive than Rebecca, who clearly had no intention of remembering Carey's name. Aunt Jane was harmless enough, whereas Rebecca put Carey in mind of a scorpion. 'Not that it wasn't a very nice little dress. I'm just surprised Jake didn't get you something more suitable.'

'I buy my own clothes,' said Carey.

'Oh yes, that's fair enough, dear, but for an occasion like this it doesn't hurt to make him get his credit card out.' Aunt Jane winked, making it impossible for Carey to dislike her.

'So, it's agreed,' said Max. 'I'll take you into town. The wedding is not until four, so there's plenty of time. I'm going riding first. Would you like to come, Carey?'

'I've never ridden a horse in my life. I

wouldn't mind looking at them though, if that's okay.'

'Come down to the stables and I'll introduce you.' Max put down his napkin. 'Maybe we can persuade Jake to give you some lessons while you're down here.'

'Actually I may be going home tomorrow.'

'Really? I thought you were staying the week.'

Carey almost made up a lie about having received an urgent message, but guilt and a bit of common sense stopped her. 'I don't think it's right that we should intrude on you too much.'

'I'll let you know if and when you've outstayed your welcome.'

'I mean it,' Carey said, as they walked to the stables together. Max had changed into jodhpurs and a white polo shirt, which showed off his honey-toned arms. She wondered if he knew just how edible he looked. 'We don't want to impose.' It was a beautiful morning with a fresh, light breeze. The sun shed dappled light on the sea. Far beneath them, on the beach, surfers were trying to catch early waves.

'Jake doesn't usually have such qualms about imposing,' said Max with a smile.

'I'm sure you'll be glad to get the house back to yourself once the wedding is over.' She almost added 'you and Rebecca', but she was afraid she might give away the secret with her tone.

'Not much chance of that with this family. As one leaves, another one arrives.' For the first time, he sounded bitter.

'I'm sorry.'

'For what?'

'That the promise you made to your dad caused you so much trouble.'

'What do you know about that?' His voice had a sharp edge.

'Aunt Jane said that he left it in his will . . . ' She tried to remember if Max had heard that bit last night. He had been so engrossed in Rebecca, he probably hadn't.

Max laughed, still sounding bitter. 'He did not leave it in his will. No, it was worse than that. It was a deathbed promise. He'd been bankrolling Jake's mother's family for fifteen years, and she forced him to make me promise it would continue.'

'Then if it's not in his will, surely you don't have to . . . '

'What the hell do you know about it, Carey?' Max stopped and turned to her, folding his arms across his broad chest. 'I spent fifteen years from the age of ten trying to get my father's attention whilst he lived in England. Look Dad, I got picked for the football team. No response. Look Dad, I made it into Harvard. No response. Look Dad, I graduated top of my class. Nothing. Only when he's dying do I get summoned here, and I thought at last he wants to know me. Maybe, I thought, he'll tell me he's been proud of me all these years. But all he wanted was to follow her orders. The woman who stole him from my mother. So I keep doing what he wants in the hopes that maybe somewhere up there he is proud of me at last.'

Carey fought a compulsion to put her arms around him and tell him all those things, but he was too angry and unapproachable at that moment. 'Jake said that your dad divorced your mum before he met his mother.'

'Jake says lots of things that aren't true, Carey. She was my father's mistress in Britain for three years before he finally divorced my mother. She . . . Diane . . . was eight months pregnant with Jake when the divorce was finalized and they married.'

'I didn't know that. I'm sorry. It must have hurt you a lot.'

'You have no idea.' Max walked on a little before stopping and looking back. 'Look, you seem like a nice kid. A bit strange and quirky, and with a slightly obsessive fixation on fitting us all into some old novel you've read, but your heart is in the right place. Just make sure Jake leaves it there when he moves on. Because he will, Carey.'

'I can take care of myself, Max.'

'You shouldn't have to. Jake should be doing that.'

'I'm a grown woman. I don't need anyone to protect me and keep me from harm.' It was Carey's turn to be angry. What was it about men and their need to dominate? 'That's just another way of controlling someone.'

'No, I think you'll find there's a difference between taking care of someone and controlling them.'

'Not in my experience.'

'Since I've told you my sob story, perhaps you want to share yours. If it's a really good one, I'll let you cry on my shoulder.' He smiled a little, as if he was trying to lighten the mood.

'No, thank you, I don't want to share it.' It would be easy to cry on his shoulder, thought Carey. It was such a strong, attractive-looking shoulder. But he had enough problems of his own, not least of which was that Jake was having an affair with Rebecca. She felt angry on Max's behalf. After all, he'd told her about striving for his father's attention. She imagined him as a young man writing those letters or emails, desperate for approval, and her heart went out to him. He deserved better than the way the Winter family treated him. 'Can . . . can we just go and see the horses now please?'

The brand-new stables were to the west of the house, about two hundred yards along the cliff, and with a huge paddock stretching inland alongside a public bridleway leading to the cliff edge. Carey inadvertently blushed when she realized that this was the direction in which Rebecca and Jake had walked the night before.

'Is something wrong?' asked Max.

'No, nothing. The horses are beautiful.' A groom was walking a big black stallion around the yard.

'He's all ready for you, Mr. Winter,' said the groom.

'Thanks, Terry.'

'Will the young lady want a horse?'

'No, thank you,' said Carey. 'I'm just here to admire them.'

'How come you've never ridden a horse?' asked Max, taking hold of the stallion's reins. It bucked a little. 'Whoa, Thor. I'm just breaking this one in. He's still a little spirited . . . ' He stopped speaking, as if he'd only just noticed the fear on Carey's face. 'You're scared of horses?'

'No, only the ones that jump around like that. I almost got thrown off one at a carnival once, when I was about eight. My mum wasn't sorry that it cured me of a My Little Pony obsession.' She smiled, trying to be brave. She didn't want him to think she was a wimp. 'It had cost her a fortune till then.'

'We'll find a nice quiet one for you tomorrow.'

'Will it have stabilisers?'

Max laughed. 'No, it won't have stabilisers. But I'm sure Jake will make sure you don't fall off. I'll be gone for about an hour. Take a look at the horses. I'll meet you back at the house.'

He mounted the stallion, and it was all Carey could do not to gasp. Man and horse together looked magnificent. With one wave, he was gone. She watched as he entered the paddock, galloping across it towards a small clutch of trees in the distance. As he did, she saw another horse and rider. It was Rebecca, and she very quickly caught up with Max, after which they rode side by side, deep in conversation. It left Carey with a heavy heart.

About an hour and a half later, Carey sat in silence in the back seat of Max's car. Rebecca had invited herself along, and she and Max spent most of the time discussing horses, which left Carey out of the conversation completely. Why it should bother Carey, she didn't know, apart from the obvious reason of knowing what Rebecca was doing behind Max's back. But it was more than that. Something she wasn't prepared to admit to herself.

'Rebecca, why don't you show Carey

where the best fashion shops are?' Max suggested once they'd parked in the busy town centre. 'Maybe you could help her to choose something.'

It was on Carey's mind to say she was quite capable of choosing her own clothes, and that the last thing she wanted was Rebecca's company or choice of clothing. She took his words as a slight, even if he had not intended them that way.

'Oh, I'm sorry, Max, darling, but I'm meeting a friend for lunch. I'm sure that if Carey stays away from the florals, she'll do fine. *Ciao.*' Rebecca waved a beautifully manicured hand, and then dashed through the traffic to the other side of the road.

'Sorry, Carey, but I need to do some business. Will you be okay?'

'I think I can find shops that sell dresses, Max. How long are you going to be? I'll meet you back here.'

They arranged to meet in about an hour. Carey wandered through Newquay, enjoying a little time alone. She was walking past a dimly lit Italian restaurant and idly stopped to read the menu board. The aroma emanating from the restaurant was mouth-watering. She was starting to feel hungry again. She glanced in through the window, wondering what it looked like inside.

Rebecca and Jake sat in a corner, wrapped in each other's arms.

4

Carey looked at her reflection in the mirror. The drop-waisted dress was gorgeous: the epitome of a summer wedding, made of organza with a pale peach pattern. Wearing it made her feel like a nineteen-twenties flapper girl. It was also way out of her price range, and would cost more than a month's salary. Could she risk putting it on her credit card? Probably not. What did it matter anyway? No one would be looking at her. Not even Max. Especially not Max. Why would he when he had Rebecca to look at? And why was she so eager to impress him anyway? She wasn't, she told herself. She just didn't want to let Jake down. That was it. Or at least that was the only self-delusion she could live with.

'It really suits you,' said the assistant, standing discreetly in the background.

'Hmm,' said Carey, thinking that the assistant would say that. The girl was no doubt on commission. 'I think I'll take the other one instead.' Her other choice, a pale green shift dress, would still cost a week's wages, but hopefully wouldn't encourage the credit-card company to send out an investigator to ask what she'd done with the normally sensible Carey Ashmore.

She turned with a sigh and saw Max standing next to the assistant, watching her. Her heart flipped. 'You look lovely,' he said. 'You should get it.'

'It's not really me,' she said, hastily returning to the changing room and hoping he hadn't seen her blushes. When she came out she paid for the green dress, wishing Max would go and do something other than watch her.

'How about lunch now?' he said when she'd finished. 'Or do you need shoes and a bag to go with the dress?'

'Nope, the ones I've got will do. Black goes with anything. Lunch would be great.'

'There's a nice little Italian place down the road . . . '

'No, not Italian!' Carey had an image of them entering the restaurant and finding Jake and Rebecca canoodling under the table. 'We'll have fish and chips. I can't come all the way to the seaside and not have fish and chips. Shall we have fish and chips?' She knew she was waffling and repeating herself, but couldn't help herself.

Max laughed. 'Okay, since you obviously feel so strongly about it, fish and chips it is. There's a seafood restaurant near the car park. I need to sort something out at the bank. Why don't you go on ahead and order?'

Carey was sure he'd already gone to the bank, but didn't think it her business to ask. 'How will I know what you want?'

'We're having fish and chips, aren't we?'

'Yes, we are.' Carey smiled with relief. 'I'll go and order then.'

Carey could see the car park from the

restaurant as she sipped her cup of tea. Max stopped there on his way back and put a carrier bag into the boot of his car. It had the name of the shop from which she'd bought her dress. She supposed he'd seen something he liked for Rebecca. Her anger grew at the way he was being deceived.

'I've ordered,' she said, a bit too brightly, when he sat down opposite her. 'But I didn't know what you wanted to drink.'

He beckoned the waitress over and asked for an espresso.

'Typical American. You're supposed to have a pot of tea with fish and chips,' Carey teased.

'Well forgive me; I didn't realise there was etiquette involved.'

'Oh yes. A cup of tea, two slices of bread and butter, salt and vinegar, and tomato ketchup. It's in the Magna Carta.'

'Wow, and our constitution only insisted on life, liberty and the pursuit of happiness.'

'That's where you Americans went wrong. You'd have had all those things if you hadn't chucked all that tea into Boston Harbor.'

'Are you okay, Carey?'

'Yes, why wouldn't I be?'

'You seem a little jumpy. I guess you're missing Jake.'

'Hardly.' On seeing his surprised expression, she added, 'What I mean is, couples don't have to be with each other all day, do they?'

'When they're in love they usually prefer not to be separated.'

'Living in someone's pocket is very overrated,' Carey said more seriously. 'Believe me, I've been there, and it's stifling.'

'This was with Dean?'

'Hmm. I think they must have gone to Grimsby to get the fish.'

'It sounds as if you had a bad time with him. Did he hurt you?' Max sounded as if his life depended on the answer, though Carey couldn't understand why it would.

'It's more complicated than that. No bruises, no apparent wounds. But . . . oh no one else believed me then, so why should you now? Even my mother thought I imagined it all.'

'Imagined what?'

'Everyone thought he was so caring. 'He looks after you,' my mum said when I complained. But it wasn't looking after me. It was controlling me. What I ate, where I went, what I wore. He chose my clothes for me towards the end. One time he took back a dress that he decided he didn't like on me, and swapped it for one more suitable.' She heard Max's sudden intake of breath but didn't really think much of it. 'And all the time he did it under the guise of caring for me. 'I only worry about you,' he used to say after he'd quizzed me for over an hour as to why I was ten minutes late getting back from my night class. It was because one of my students had a crisis and needed advice, but he wouldn't accept that answer. Then he'd undermine me. The way I looked, the things I said. But always in a disingenuous way, like: 'I think it would be much better if you wore your hair this way,' and, 'That dress doesn't suit you, and I know you don't want to go out looking like an idiot. Not that I'm saying you look like an idiot, sweetheart.' It was all so . . . so insidious, and . . . ' Carey stopped, realising that she'd said more about Dean to Max than she'd even said to her own mother. Part of the reason was that her mother could see no wrong in her ex. 'Probably very boring.'

'Not at all. It obviously hurt you.' It was only when Max said it, that Carey realised she had tears in her eyes. She brushed them away impatiently. She couldn't understand why the words kept coming. Something about Max drew them from her. 'I'm not hurt, because by the end any feelings I had for him died. He killed them. More than anything it frightened me. I felt that I was losing myself. And whilst he hasn't hurt me physically, the last time I saw him there was something there that set the alarm bells ringing. As if he'd tried all other ways to control me and that was going to be next. It wasn't anything he said or did. Just a feeling I had. But no one believes me. He still goes to see my mother, to find out what I'm up to. And she tells him because she thinks he's harmlessly in love with me and she's swept up in the romance of it all. Oh, here's the food. I won't have to cry on your shoulder any more now.'

'I don't mind. It explains a little about you and Jake . . . I think.'

'What do you mean? I know we're not exactly love's young dream, but . . . '

'Let's eat,' he said, frowning and picking up his knife and fork. 'Forget about everything else for a while.'

They chatted happily over lunch, finding that they enjoyed many of the same films and books, as well as liking some of the same music. Carey couldn't remember the last time she'd enjoyed a man's company so much. Max talked to her, not at her, and it made a noticeable difference to how she felt in his company. She began to relax and laugh, and forgot to worry so much about what he thought of her.

Everything was fine until they got to his car and opened the boot so she could put her shopping bags inside. As she leaned in, she caught a glimpse of the material inside the carrier bag he'd put in earlier. It was the expensive dress she'd been trying on. So that was what he'd bought for Rebecca. There was no reason why he shouldn't. It was a nice dress. Yet to Carey it felt like a slap in the face. Rebecca, who towered above her, would look fabulous in it. He'd obviously been thinking that whilst watching her preen in front of the mirror. She smiled tightly at him, deciding to say nothing. Their drive home was much quieter than their lunchtime chat, with Carey only able to answer in monosyllables when Max spoke to her. She knew she was being childish. It was none of her business what he bought for his girlfriend, but deep down she ached with some emotion she could not name.

The family had started to assemble at the house, ready to make their way to the wedding. Carey rushed upstairs to change, trying hard not to think about the bag in the boot of Max's car which, for some reason, he'd left there when she'd taken hers out. She chastised herself silently. She was being silly. It was only a dress after all. The green shift dress was good enough. It gave her a bit of a nineteen-fifties look. These were all the things she told herself as she looked at herself in the mirror and, in reality, found she was sadly wanting. No, that was silly. The dress looked okay on her, even if it wasn't what she'd really wanted, and at least it wouldn't take too long to clear her credit card. She fixed a smile on her face and went downstairs.

'What a nice little dress, dear,' said Aunt Jane. Carey could have kissed her. 'Very Audrey Hepburn.'

'That's a kind thing to say, thank you,' said Carey, genuinely smiling. 'She was wonderful.'

'Oh yes. They don't make them like her anymore. Gamine, that's what she was. You're not quite as gamine. More hourglass, but it still looks good on you. Jake, doesn't Carey look pretty?' There was an edge to Aunt Jane's voice. Jake was standing in the corner, whispering to Rebecca.

'What? Oh yeah. Gorgeous.' Jake walked across and was about to kiss Carey on the lips, but she turned her head and he got her cheek instead. She was angry with him on Max's behalf, even whilst believing none of it was her concern. She felt a guilty pang. No, it wasn't her business and she had no right to tell Max what she'd seen. A little voice told her that she couldn't trust her motives for doing so. But it might be worth having a word with Jake and suggesting he be a bit more discreet. Yes, she'd do that later. It would ease her conscience, even if it did nothing to put an end to the affair.

'It's amazing what you can get in these supermarkets nowadays, isn't it?' said Rebecca sweetly. She wore a floaty white chiffon dress and a wide-brimmed hat. Carey was pretty sure that no one but the bride should wear all white, but she supposed Rebecca had her own rules. She paused to wonder why Rebecca wasn't wearing the dress that Max bought.

Guests stood around chatting informally, when Max came in and announced that the cars had arrived. Carey's heart gave a lurch. He looked breathtakingly handsome in a grey morning suit.

Carey and Jake were moving towards the door when Rebecca, carrying a glass of red wine, bumped into them, spilling wine all over Carey's green dress. 'Oh, I'm so clumsy,' she said. 'I am so sorry, Clara.' It occurred to Carey that if Rebecca got her name wrong once more, she might just slap her. 'It looks like you'll have to get the floral maxi-dress out again.'

'It's no problem,' said Carey. 'I . . . erm . . . I'll catch you all up.' She dashed upstairs, fighting back the tears. She had no doubt that Rebecca had done it on purpose just to humiliate her. Rather than change, she wished she could get on the next train home.

She was half undressed when there was a knock on the door and it opened. She pulled the dress back up so it just covered her bra but left her shoulders bare.

'Sorry,' said Max. He walked into the room, carrying the bag from the shop. 'Look, I wasn't going to give you this after what you said about Dean.' He sounded bashful in a way that Carey found incredibly sexy. 'I don't want you to think that I'm trying to tell you what to wear or anything. But you looked real pretty in it and I guessed the price tag put you off so I thought I'd surprise you. Then you told me all that stuff about Dean at lunch and I was afraid you'd be annoyed with me. So I was going to take it back on Monday. It won't fit anyone else and it's not quite my style.' He smiled. 'I'll put the bag on the bed.' He matched the action to the words. 'And you can wear it if you want, or not if you don't want to. I'm not telling you what to do, Carey.'

'Max, you shouldn't have done that . . . ' She choked back the tears that were threatening to fall. 'I mean, I'm really grateful and I would like to wear it but . . . it cost a fortune and you barely know me.'

'Call it an engagement gift if you prefer.' His voice took on a grim note. 'If it makes you feel happier about wearing it, that is.' He ran his fingers through his hair in a way that was becoming very familiar and endearing to her. 'I've sent the others ahead. I'll wait for you downstairs.'

'Thank you.'

5

The church was a pretty little building of Norman origin and had been decorated with flowers. The scent wafted through the church. A string quartet played as the bride walked down the aisle on the arm of her father. Choirboys led everyone through the hymns, covering up the less-than-angelic tones of the guests. It was a pity the string quartet had to compete with the sound of rock music coming from a funfair about a mile from the church but Carey supposed one could not have everything, even at the perfect wedding.

There was no doubt that Stephanie and Tristan made a very attractive couple. A local paper was covering the wedding, as they were apparently local celebrities; Stephanie had won several local beauty contests and Tristan was the son of a celebrated racehorse owner. It crossed Carey's mind to wonder why Tristan and Rebecca's father hadn't contributed to the wedding. She couldn't help noticing that things were somewhat frosty between them and Jake's family, and she wondered why that might be. Perhaps they weren't happy about Tristan marrying Stephanie. But after the wedding was over, Tristan's parents hugged Stephanie warmly enough. Whatever put the families at loggerheads, it wasn't the newlyweds.

The hotel was only a short drive from the church, and was something of a revelation to Carey. It was what she'd expected Max's house to be: a large Gothic pile overlooking the sea, and with its own private beach. It had clearly been intended for the luxury market. Inside it was sumptuous and comfortable, with waiters on hand with drinks seconds before anyone decided they were thirsty.

The food was delicious, cooked by a well-known television chef especially for the occasion, though Carey couldn't help thinking that she'd preferred the fish and chips she ate with Max at lunchtime. Thinking of him, she looked for him and noticed how he sat apart from everyone else. Aunt Jane sat near to him and chatted to him occasionally, but for the most part he was alone. She wished she could go and talk to him, because she felt alone too. Jake had gone to dance with one of the bridesmaids. Wrapped in an embrace with the girl on the dance floor, he had more or less forgotten Carey was there. Not that she cared about that. She tried chatting to a man on her right, who was drinking heavily and looking at Rebecca intently as she danced with the best man.

'Are you one of Jake's relatives?' she asked him.

'Ralph Wareham,' he said, holding out his hand. 'Rebecca's ex. Tristan and I were at school together.' He would have been a good-looking guy if not for the bloodshot eyes.

'Oh . . . is erm . . . is that your wife dancing with Tristan?'

'God no. I'm never going there again. Once was enough. She's my girlfriend and I've told her she'll stay that way. Who are you?'

Carey thought he seemed a bit rude, but put it down to the drink. 'I'm Carey Ashmore. Jake's . . . fiancée.'

'Are you, now? Well that's interesting. Got engaged just before you came, did you?'

'Yes, how did you know that?'

'It's par for the course. Let me give you a bit of advice, Carrie . . . ' At least Ralph was closer than the others when it came to her name.

'It's pronounced Care-y.'

'Whatever. Run, girl. Run as fast as you can. They'll poison you between them. That's what they always do with people. They thrive on hurting each other and don't care who else gets hurt in the meantime.'

'I don't think I understand . . . '

Ralph Wareham laughed harshly. 'You

will, girl. You will.'

'Who do you mean?'

'Hi, Ralph. How are you?' Max sat down in an empty seat opposite them.

'Max, my old pal, how goes it? Now this is a good guy, Carey. Yeah, Max is okay. The only one in these two godforsaken families who is.'

'I hope you're not telling Carey any horror stories, Ralph.'

'Someone has to tell her, Max. She's a pretty little thing. They always are though, aren't they? Pretty but ordinary-looking so they don't give the goddess too much to worry about.' Ralph took another gulp of his beer. 'Jake's fiancées. Note the plural.'

'That's enough now, Ralph. Would you like to dance, Carey?' The way he asked suggested that it was more of a command than a question.

Max held Carey close as they moved around the dance floor to a slow song. She was hyper-aware of his strong arm on her waist, his solid chest muscles and the aroma of his expensive cologne.

'What did Ralph mean about Jake's fiancées, plural?' she asked after a minute or two.

'Try not to worry about it now.' Max spoke gently. 'Let's just enjoy the dance.'

'I think I have a right to know,' she said, even though in reality she didn't. But Max didn't know that. Not for the first time, Carey had the sense of an underlying story to everything that was going on.

'Yes, you're probably right. But it might upset you, and I'm sure you don't want to spoil Stephanie and Tristan's day.' He sounded strained, and as if that wasn't the real reason. She sensed he was afraid of upsetting her. It made her feel safe there, in his arms. As if nothing ever could hurt her whilst she was with him. The feeling also frightened her. She didn't want to rely on anyone, not after Dean. She wanted to be her own person. But dancing in Max's arms, feeling him close to her, his strong jaw-line only inches from her lips, it would be so easy to become his. She reminded herself that he didn't want her. He had Rebecca. Or so he thought. It was ironic. He clearly didn't want to hurt her, and she definitely didn't want to hurt him. It rendered them both speechless.

'No, of course not.'

'I'm sorry; I didn't mean to sound as if I was chastising you, Carey.'

'Don't worry, you didn't. But once today is over, let's be honest with each other, shall we?' She was asking for something she wasn't even sure she could give. Never mind that she'd lied to him about being Jake's fiancée; how could she tell him about Jake and Rebecca? He deserved so much better.

'Why? Have you been lying to me about something?' Was it her imagination, or did he sound hopeful?

'No, no, of course not.' She had the grace to blush at the out-and-out lie. 'I mean about the things we're not telling each other. The things you're not telling me about Jake, I suppose.'

'Would you hate me if I said that I wanted to do everything I could to protect you from being hurt?'

'I'm a big girl, Max. But no, I could never hate you. I believe that everything you do, you genuinely do for the best.'

She looked up at him and for what seemed like a lifetime, their eyes locked. Everyone else drifted away, and it was as if they had the dance floor to themselves. Only they existed in the whole world. He moved his head a little so that their lips were within an inch of each other. She waited for, longed for, the kiss that would surely follow. The music stopped and everyone started clapping, breaking the spell. But still he held her close to him. 'Are you cold?' he asked.

'No.'

'You're trembling.'

'Am I?' She was actually feeling quite warm. Hot even.

'Not trying to steal my girl, are you, Max?' asked Jake, nudging them.

'Someone will if you don't take better care of her,' said Max through thin lips. He unceremoniously let Carey go and walked away.

Jake took Max's place, putting his arms around Carey's waist. 'Are you enjoying yourself, Carey?'

'I was,' she said glumly. 'I need to speak to you.'

'What about? If it's about not staying in the hotel, I've already told you, it's beyond my control. Max is the boss. In all things.'

'That's not the impression I get from him, Jake. In fact he just seems like a nice guy who has found himself responsible for people who despise him.'

'Oh don't let Max fool you. He seems decent enough, but really he uses his money to control us all. Rebecca tells me he only bought you that dress because he didn't think the one you had was good enough.'

'Really?' Carey felt her heart sink. Had Max manipulated her into wearing it? All that stuff about not wanting to control her. Had it been a way of making her do exactly what he said? No, it didn't make sense. He couldn't possibly have known Rebecca was going to tip wine over her. Unless they planned it. Carey's head spun. Things were becoming far too complicated. 'Is all this stuff about Max being the bad guy what you tell yourself to ease your guilt about sleeping with his girlfriend?' She hit out at Jake because he was the only one there, but her words had the desired effect. He pushed her away from him and glared at her angrily. He looked from Max to Rebecca and back again with a quizzical expression in his eyes. Rebecca was dancing with Ralph, which surprised Carey after everything he'd said about his ex-wife. The woman had power over men, even those who claimed to despise her.

'Keep your nose out of things that don't concern you, Carey.'

'Oh don't worry, Jake,' she hissed. Luckily her words were drowned by the music. 'I will. I'm going home tomorrow, whether you've got your trust fund or not. I've had enough of you and your family.'

She stormed from the ballroom and went outside onto the hotel terrace. There were a few people sitting at the tables, so she walked to the end where there was some decking and a low railing with a view out to the sea. The cliff wasn't quite as steep as the one behind Max's house. Wooden steps led down to the hotel's private beach. With a sudden pressing need to get away, Carey walked down the steps, slipping off her shoes en route.

The early evening sun shone down and the sand was still warm. She pressed her toes into it, the heat on her feet acting like a soothing massage. Walking further down the beach, she found a large rock and sat on it looking out to sea. It was close enough so that the tide could run over her feet, making a pleasantly cool contrast with the heat of the sand. Gradually she began to feel calmer. She still hated Jake for spoiling the pleasure she'd felt when Max had given her the dress. She'd wanted to believe it was a genuine gesture from a genuine man. Now she wasn't so sure. Why would Max buy her a dress anyway? A little voice told her that he'd only done it to make her happy, but her experience with Dean had made her suspicious of anyone's motives where she was concerned. Max probably bought it because he'd seen her in the cheaper one she'd chosen and found her wanting.

As before, she felt as if she'd stepped into a mystery. Not a murder, thankfully, but something to do with family secrets. There was a definite atmosphere between both sides of the family. She sensed they were putting on a brave face for the wedding. They spoke politely to each other but with no real warmth. She didn't know anyone well enough to ask, and those she did know spoke cryptically: Max because he said he didn't want to hurt her; Jake because he was hiding something from Max and perhaps didn't trust her enough. She guessed that Aunt Jane might be the one to tell it like it really was, especially after a drink or two, but she hadn't had much chance to talk to the old lady all day.

She told herself she was being silly. At other weddings she attended, there had been a definite demarcation of family lines, with the bride's family and friends on one side and the groom's family on the other. Not just in the church but at the reception. But there had also been a thawing towards the evening when drink loosened everyone up, and the ice had been broken by something or other. People didn't exactly part as the best of friends, but briefly they let down the barriers and found common ground in the happy couple. There was none of that at this wedding. She had the distinct impression that once the wedding was over, there would be a parting of the ways and they'd never be in the same room again if they could possibly help it.

Whilst Carey had no proof, she had the strong suspicion that it was to do with Rebecca. She pushed the thought aside as being uncharitable. She didn't like Rebecca, but it was no reason to blame her for everything. Carey was only jealous because Rebecca was . . . because Rebecca was Max's girlfriend. The realisation hit her like a ten-ton truck and felt just as painful.

'Carey?' Almost as if thinking of him had summoned him up, she heard Max's voice behind her. She turned to look at him and saw that he'd taken his tie off. Standing on the beach with his shirt open to reveal a few fine chest hairs, and his hands in his pockets, he looked like the model from an advert for expensive aftershave. She didn't realize until then that men with such latent masculinity and sex appeal existed in real life. Even in the pretty dress he'd bought her, she looked down and found herself wanting.

'Oh, hi . . . '

'You okay?'

'What? Yes, fine. Just enjoying the view. You're very lucky to have this beach all to yourself. It's lovely, isn't it? Like a bit of paradise.'

'I don't exactly have it to myself. It's for the guests.'

'Yes, of course.'

'Are you thinking you'd rather have stayed at the hotel?'

'Oh no, no, not at all. I'm grateful to you for putting up with us. I mean putting us up. I mean . . . ' She didn't know what she meant, only that she was waffling like an idiot, just in case he could see right into her mind and know exactly what she was thinking about him at that moment. What she was really thinking was how much she would like to rip his shirt off and cover his muscular chest in kisses.

'Did you and Jake have a row?'

'You could say that. I'm going home tomorrow.'

'We're supposed to be going horse-riding in the morning. Remember?'

'Oh, yes. Perhaps some other time.'

'Is there going to be another time, Carey? I can't help thinking that if I let you walk out of here now I'm never going to see you again.'

'That'll be a relief for you then.'

She heard him hiss through his teeth. 'Now why would you think that?'

'I don't. I mean . . . Oh ignore me. I don't know what I mean.'

'Is it over between you and Jake?'

She didn't know how to answer that. Part of her still felt some loyalty to Jake's original scheme, even if she felt just as guilty about deceiving Max. 'Who knows? We probably rushed things a bit.'

'I'm inclined to agree with that. Except . . . '

'What?'

'It's none of my business, but you hardly seem like a couple at all.'

'Well like I said, we're not exactly love's young dream.'

'You're not love's young anything,' Max said, sounding annoyed. 'I don't like being lied to, Carey.'

She stood up, overwhelmed by guilt. It came out as anger. 'Well perhaps if you didn't spend your life trying to control people they wouldn't feel the need to lie to you.'

'What the hell is that supposed to mean?'

'I know you only bought me this dress because you didn't think what I was wearing was good enough. Rebecca told Jake.'

'What does Rebecca know about it? I'm sorry I dared to do something nice for you, Carey. I won't be making that mistake again. Not when you consider every act of kindness as a means of enslaving you.'

'I'm sorry, I didn't mean . . . '

'Yeah, yeah, you don't know what you mean. That's pretty much your get-out clause for everything, isn't it? Well, when you finally work it out, let me know. Because I know for a fact something is going on here and if you're a party to it all then you're not the person I think you are.'

'What are you talking about? Party to what?' Carey felt her cheeks redden. Why she should be surprised he'd worked out Jake's plot, she didn't know. She'd felt all along it was a lame idea, and Max was a clever man.

'So you are in on it. Don't deny it, Carey. I can see it in your face.' He looked at her with disgust then turned away and stormed up the beach. Controlled fury emanated from him, in the line of his shoulders and the way he held his head. Suddenly he turned and came back to her, spitting out angry words. 'I knew it was all fake. It was a lousy performance by the way. You're not lovers. You don't behave like lovers. Damn it, you don't even kiss like lovers.'

Carey put her hands on her hips. 'Oh, and how exactly are lovers supposed to kiss?' She knew she shouldn't have asked the question the moment she said it.

With one swift movement Max's

arms were around her and he'd covered her mouth with his, taking complete possession of her. Instead of pushing him away, which was what she should have done, she found herself returning the kiss with enthusiasm. She'd never been kissed like it, and probably never would be again. A small devil within her decided to enjoy the moment, even though she knew he was only making a point. The kiss meant nothing to him, whilst it excited her beyond all rational thought, allowing the imp in her to take over and wind her arms around his neck, curling his hair around her fingers. He thrust his tongue between her parted lips, sending a bolt of electricity through her body.

He held her away from him angrily, his hands burning into the bare skin of her shoulders.

'That's how lovers kiss.'

Then he turned and walked away.

6

Carey lay awake in the dark, replaying the kiss over and over in her mind. If that was how lovers kissed, she'd obviously been missing out on a lot in her life. In her fantasy the kiss continued and led to them rolling in the sand, entwined in each other's bodies. No matter how hard she tried not to think of it, the memory kept returning.

Max had walked away, leaving her standing there with a stunned expression on her face. She had no idea how she'd got through the evening. It had gone by in a blur. She only noticed that he had disappeared, and he didn't show his face for the rest of the night.

In a way that was a blessing. She didn't know how she'd be able to face him. The kiss had confirmed what she had been trying to deny all along. As if life wasn't complicated enough, she was falling in love with him.

How could he have kissed her like that whilst despising her? It hurt her to think about it. The kiss had been the best thing to ever happen to her, and perversely, the worst thing to ever happen to her.

She would have to leave the next day. She couldn't bear to see him again.

When she did go downstairs in the morning, it was to find Max and Jake involved in some argument. 'If she's really your fiancée then you should come,' Max was saying. 'You've spent precious little time with her.'

'I don't want to go riding,' said Jake. 'I've got other things to do.'

'I'm sure you have, but you are coming with us. Oh, Carey, there you are. We're just about to go riding before breakfast.'

'I'm not bothered, actually . . . '

'The horses are ready,' said Max. 'It isn't fair to put the grooms to so much trouble for no reason.'

'Oh, no, I suppose not.' She meekly

followed the two men to the stable. She might just as well have been invisible for the attention they paid her. Both were deep in thought, and both angry — with each other and, she guessed, with her for being there.

When they reached the stable, Max climbed onto his black horse. Jake's horse was a brown thoroughbred stallion, whilst Carey's could only have answered to the name 'Dobbin'. It was old but, she had to admit, very sweet with soft dark eyes. He nuzzled her cheek, and she was relieved that someone there liked her.

Neither of the men offered to help her mount Dobbin. It was left to the groom to assist her. She saw Max flash a furious glance at Jake, but Jake wasn't looking in her direction, or at least was pretending hard not to.

'Keep hold of the reins,' Max told Jake.

'What's that? Like a stabilizer?' said Carey, trying to lighten the mood.

'Something like that. Jake, are you

going to tell Carey what she needs to do?'

'Yes, show me the ignition,' she said, her quip falling on deaf ears. She felt like telling them where to put their horses, but good manners and a fear of bursting into tears prevented her.

Jake half-heartedly took her through some commands, showing her how to use the reins to keep the horse in check.

'We'll stick to the bridleway,' said Max, 'and we'll go slow.'

The bridleway ran parallel to the main road. As nervous as she felt, Carey quite enjoyed riding Dobbin. The two brothers rode in silence, and for a change she managed not to fill the silence with senseless chatter, which was her usual habit when in awkward situations.

'So, when's the wedding?' Max said after they'd travelled several hundred yards from the stables. 'You can hold it here if you wish.'

'What wedding?' asked Carey.

'He means ours,' said Jake. 'We'll

probably wait a while, since it was all so sudden. Won't we, darling?'

So that was it. Jake had convinced Max that they were really engaged. Why it made Carey angry, after Max finding out the truth had left her feeling embarrassed and humiliated, she didn't know. But it did mean that in Max's opinion, she was engaged to Jake when she let him kiss her. And she did let him. The truth of that burned inside her. That she knew she had no real reason to feel ashamed didn't help at all. It was what Max thought that bothered her.

'I'm not bothered,' she said glumly, when she realized that they were both waiting for an answer.

'Oh come on, you two,' said Max. 'You had a tiff and now it's over. Why don't you kiss and make up?' There was a challenge in his voice.

'I don't want to be kissed at this moment,' said Carey. 'Not by anyone. I'm too busy trying to make Dobbin like me.' She saw the corners of Max's mouth curl up.

'Dobbin?'

'Yes.'

'His name is Thunderbolt.'

'No, really? Are you sure?'

'He was a racehorse in his younger days.'

'Oh.' She patted the horse. 'Sorry, Thunderbolt. I didn't mean to impugn your horsey skills.'

Jake tutted.

'What's your problem?' she asked.

'Nothing, it's just . . . well you're so ditzy sometimes, Carey, that's all.'

'It's a good job you don't have to put up with me for much longer then.'

'So no kissing and making up today,' said Max.

'I've got a better idea. Why don't you two kiss and make up? Because brothers should stick together and not . . . ' She almost said 'not steal each other's girlfriends'. 'Really, you act like a couple of ten-year-olds, fighting over a train set. Or in this case, your father's money.'

'My father's money . . . ?' Max frowned.

'Well it isn't fair that you hold back Jake's trust fund,' said Carey.

'Shut up, Carey,' said Jake.

'He's a grown-up and should be able to make his own mistakes.'

To her amazement Max laughed out loud at that. He tapped his horse with his feet and took off across the field.

'I told you to keep your nose out of things that don't concern you,' said Jake.

'Do you know your family's problem?' said Carey.

'No, but I'm sure you're going to tell me.'

'You don't talk to each other. You creep around with your secrets and lies, but you don't actually come out and say what you're really thinking. Well except Aunt Jane, and she's drunk most of the time so it doesn't count. It was about time someone brought it out into the open.'

'It was between me and Max. Ergo, none of your business.'

'You made it my business when you asked me to take part in this charade, Jake. Last night Max had worked out that we weren't really engaged. You should have left it like that, but oh no, you've got to have your little intrigues, haven't you?' It struck Carey that she'd never said a truer word, and that maybe she'd hit on the key to something. But the feeling passed by quickly because it didn't make sense.

'What did Max work out? What did you say? What did he say?' Jake stopped his horse and glared at her.

'He said he knew what we were up to, that it was written all over my face. So I didn't bother denying it, because quite frankly I've decided I don't owe you any more loyalty. If I ever did.'

'And you took that to mean that he was talking about the trust fund?'

'Well, yes, what else?'

'Nothing. Come on, we'll go to the end of the bridleway and then I'll walk you back. I've got to go out later.'

'How am I supposed to get home?'

'I don't know. Get a train or something.'

'Thanks, Jake. You bring me here, full of dreams and schemes, and when it doesn't work out as you want it to, you expect me to pay my own way home.'

'I'm not leaving here. Not at the moment. I need to find out what's happening with Max and Rebecca.'

'In what way?'

'Never mind . . . '

'If you say it's none of my business again, I'm going to . . . ' Carey stopped, because she wasn't really the violent type. 'You're paying for my train ticket home, Jake. It's the least you can do after I spent money I couldn't really afford on a dress that Rebecca ruined.'

They rode towards the end of the bridleway. As they did, the traffic on the road alongside it became busier, with holiday-makers emerging from their cottages and making their way to the beach or local attractions.

With the argument at an end, Carey quite enjoyed riding Thunderbolt. She still preferred to think of him as Dobbin, though she wasn't quite sure if that was some sort of racism against horses. She wished she was a good enough rider to take off across the fields like Max. She pushed away the idea that she really wanted to ride off in pursuit of Max. He didn't want her anyway. He'd made that much clear by insisting to Jake she was his fiancée, and then making his brother take responsibility for her.

They were near to the end of the bridleway when Jake suddenly exclaimed, 'There's Rebecca!' He let go of the reins on Carey's horse and galloped across the field, leaving Carey sitting open-mouthed on Thunderbolt.

'Jake! Jake, don't leave me. I can't ride alone . . . I . . . ' In her panic at being left alone, she'd forgotten everything that Jake had told her earlier about how to make Thunderbolt do what she wanted. 'It's okay . . . er . . . Dobbin . . . ' she said, patting his neck. 'We can do this, can't we?' She moved the reins and succeeded in turning Thunderbolt around so he was at least facing back towards the stables. So far so good. She patted him lightly with her heels and he started walking slowly in that direction. 'There. Good boy. Now don't drop me or anything.' In her initial shock at being alone, it hadn't occurred to her to get off him. Now she wondered if she should. Or even if she could. She was rather short and he was a big horse.

Deciding it was the best thing to do, so she could safely walk him back to the stables, she took one foot out of the stirrup and started to dismount. At the same time a car on the road backfired, the exhaust bursting like a pistol shot. Before Carey had chance to realize what was happening, Thunderbolt reared up and then started running hell-for-leather along the bridleway, whilst all Carey could do was hang on for dear life. She tried to get her foot back into the stirrup in order to regain some control, but he was moving too fast for her, throwing her body about. 'Stop!' she cried. 'Please, stop.' She felt herself sliding down, and for one horrible moment thought she might fall under him and end up being trampled. 'Dobbin . . . Thunderbolt, please stop.' She was vaguely aware of the sound of galloping slightly out of step with Thunderbolt, but in her terror didn't think much of it. The car that backfired must have been travelling in the same direction, because it backfired again. Thunderbolt reared upwards.

Just when Carey thought she'd be thrown to the ground, she felt safe arms enfolding her waist, and pulling her off Thunderbolt and onto another horse. He held her close to him and gradually brought his horse to a stop. Thunderbolt was still galloping off into the distance, towards the stables. 'Oh, Max,' she sobbed into his shoulder, her whole body trembling.

'Shh, it's okay. You're safe now.' Even though he spoke in soothing tones, she noticed that his body was tense with anger. She looked up and saw that anger written in his face. He said nothing until they got to the stables and helped her down. When her legs almost buckled under her, he caught her and helped her to a bench at the far end of the stable block, where he sat her down. By the time they reached it, she wasn't altogether sure if the trembling didn't have more to do with Max holding her. He left her there for a few minutes to go and speak to the groom.

'Where's Jake?' he asked when he returned.

'He saw . . . someone,' she said. 'And just took off.'

'Rebecca, I suppose.'

'Yes. Sorry.' Did he know, she wondered.

Max paced in front of her. 'He's a damned idiot leaving you like that. When I think of what could have happened . . . Why didn't you get off the horse, Carey?'

'Oh so it's my fault, is it?'

'I'm not saying that. Only that you should have.'

'I wasn't thinking, all right?' She stood up, trying to ignore that her knees still seemed to be made of jelly. 'First you took off, then Jake, and I was left there on my own, and I was flummoxed. I didn't know what to do for the best. And it's not my fault a car backfired! Twice!' She felt tears sting her eyes. She was sick of all the lies and the games and somehow always ending up as the one who was in the wrong.

'No, of course not. I'm sorry. It's just that when I saw Thunderbolt rear up, I thought you were going to be hurt.' He sounded choked, then angry again. 'Jake should take better care of you.'

'I can take care of myself!'

'Oh yeah, I could see that. You had it all under control. Right up until the horse nearly threw you.'

'Is the horse okay?'

'What?' Her question seemed to take him aback.

'The horse. Dobbin . . . Thunderbolt.

Is he okay? He was really scared and . . .'

Max looked heavenward before laughing incredulously. 'Just when I think you can't surprise me any more, Carey Ashmore, you do. Yes, he's fine. The groom has put him back in the stable. There's a reason he's called Thunderbolt, by the way.'

'Why?'

'Normally he's very placid, but he doesn't like loud noises, particularly thunderstorms. That's why we had to retire him. That starting pistol wasn't his best friend. I didn't think there'd be any problems today, with the sky being so clear. A car backfiring didn't occur to me. Come on, let's go back to the house and have some breakfast.' Just as they were walking back, Jake and Rebecca returned. 'You go ahead,' said Max. 'I want to talk to Jake.'

Carey was nosey enough to wish she could remain, but as it wasn't any of her business, she did as Max asked.

She was alone all through breakfast,

as Aunt Jane and the other house-guests had theirs in bed. Max didn't return and neither did Jake and Rebecca. She briefly saw Max through the front window, getting into his car and driving away. A few minutes later, Jake ran through the hall and up the stairs. She didn't see him come back down, but heard the front door slam ten minutes later. She went to the window and saw him get into his car with Rebecca before driving away, too.

'Great,' she muttered, feeling a bit sorry for herself.

'Have you finished in here, Miss Ashmore?' asked Sheila, the house-keeper. She was completely unlike the sinister Mrs. Danvers. Sheila was in her fifties and motherly-looking, with sym-pathetic brown eyes.

'Yes. Sorry to have kept you waiting, Sheila.'

'Oh, not at all. You haven't eaten much.'

'I know. I'm a bit off my food. But what I did have was lovely. Do you know where Jake has gone?'

'I'm sorry, I . . . ' Sheila looked behind her as if afraid of being caught out. 'No, I'm sorry, I don't. If there's anything else you need, do let me know.' Sheila bustled about putting things on trays.

'A bit of the truth wouldn't go amiss.'

'Excuse me?' The housekeeper put a coffee cup onto the tray and paused.

'Oh, nothing. And I shouldn't ask you to talk about your employers anyway.'

'Between you and me, it's a strange sort of family. But in the years I've been doing this, I've never really worked for a normal family.' Sheila smiled. 'Max is okay, though. I wasn't sure when he first took over from his father. A new broom and all that. But if I'm perfectly honest, it's been much nicer working here since Jake's mother passed on. She was a bit above herself if you ask me. Treated servants like dirt, even though her grandmother was in service with my grandmother years ago, so we're from the same class. Not that I've got anything against people bettering themselves. I just wish they'd remember where they came from. It's an odd thing, but people born into money, like Max, tend to be better with their staff. More civil. You get someone *nouveau riche*, as they call them, and they think that the lord or lady of the manor has to act imperious and bossy.'

'You like Max a lot, don't you?'

'If the truth be known . . . ' Sheila winked. 'If I was twenty years younger, I'd be setting my cap at him.'

Carey laughed. 'I think Rebecca might have something to say about that.'

'Rebecca Wareham? Oh I don't think so. You're barking up the wrong tree there, dear.'

'She is his girlfriend.'

'She's tried to be a few times, usually when . . . ' Sheila clamped her mouth shut. 'There, I've said too much again. I'd best get these pots back to the kitchen. They won't walk there themselves.'

'Can I help?'

'No . . . ' Sheila smiled warmly. 'No, now don't go taking on anything I've said as an insult to yourself or a hint that you should be helping me. You're a nice girl. Everyone can see that.'

'Sheila?' said Carey as the housekeeper walked towards the door.

'What, dear?'

'I'm sorry if I ever thought you'd be like Mrs. Danvers.'

Sheila laughed out loud. 'Thanks to that film, everyone thinks housekeepers are like her. Oh Lawrence Olivier . . . He was edible in that, wasn't he?' A look of realization flashed on her face. 'Of course, that's what you're getting at! Maxim de Winter . . . Max Winter. Would you believe it's never occurred to me till this moment? I'm obviously getting old.'

'No, not you.'

'Like I said, everyone thinks you're a nice girl.'

Carey was about to go upstairs and pack when she heard a car backfire again, but it seemed much closer. She went to the door and opened it, to see an old Citroën parked at the front of the house. Before the driver's door opened and he started to get out, her blood felt chilled. She hugged her arms around her for warmth, but it was futile. A man of medium height got out. He was slightly balding, and stocky, but good-looking in a blokey sort of way.

'Carey, darling . . . ' he said, holding his arms open.

'Hello, Dean,' she said, starting to tremble all over her body. 'What do you want?'

7

'Are you going to ask me in?' Dean walked towards the front door and Carey instinctively backed off.

'I can't. This isn't my house.'

'Let's go for a drive then.'

'No. I'm just about to pack to go home.'

'Then I can take you there. I told your mother I'd get you home safely.'

'I don't have to ask how you found out where I was.' Dean always had been able to charm her mother, convincing her that Carey imagined things. He told her what every mother wanted to hear: that he only had Carey's best interests at heart.

'Carey, darling, your mother understands how it is between us. She said you'd gone off to Cornwall with some Winter bloke.' It only then occurred to Carey that Dean didn't know Jake

Winter. Jake had only been working at the centre a few weeks when she broke up with Dean, and because she'd been afraid of Dean's response, she'd deliberately not mentioned she'd helped her old university friend to get a job. 'Then when I got here yesterday . . . '

'Yesterday? You were here?'

'That's right. I came yesterday. When I got here, I found out some stupid story about how you'd gone and got engaged.'

'Who told you that?' Carey still stood in front of the door, not wanting him to pass through it, but terrified that if he came any closer he'd be able to touch her, and she didn't want that. The trembling sensation in her body was completely opposite to how it felt when Max touched her. With him she trembled with longing and anticipation. With Dean it was as if a cold, slimy hand touched her spine and wouldn't let go.

'Some old woman. Said she was an aunty here.' Carey guessed he meant

Aunt Jane, but wondered why Jane hadn't mentioned it. 'She was a bit drunk,' Dean said, answering the question. 'And I asked her not to say anything. I wanted my visit to be a surprise.'

'Well it's certainly that. So now you can turn around and go away again.'

'Carey, darling, you need me, even if you don't admit it to yourself. I mean, look at the silly, impulsive things you do. Like going off and getting yourself engaged to someone you barely know.'

'That's not true. I've known him since we were at university.'

'Did you sleep with him then?' There was the Dean she feared. The one who she was sure would one day become dangerous. His voice was as cold as steel.

'That's none of your business.'

'So you did.' Dean sighed. Carey knew it would be useless to deny it. He wouldn't believe her anyway. Dean believed whatever he needed to believe in order to put her down. 'But I forgive you.'

'Forgive me? You've no right to forgive me! I don't have to account to you for any man I might have slept with before we met! Or since, for that matter.'

'No, darling. Of course not. But if our relationship is going to work, we have to be honest with each other.'

'Okay, this is me being honest. We don't have a relationship. I don't love you. I never did. And now I want you to go away and leave me alone.'

'I can't do that. Your mother's relying on me to keep you on the straight and narrow. Like I said, I'm willing to forgive you for this . . . aberration, but I will have to set some ground rules if we're to stay together.'

'Have you heard a word I've said? We are not together. We are never going to be together. You're the one who needs to get back on the straight and narrow. Go away and get counselling, but don't expect me to be a part of your life.'

Dean stepped forward, and at the same time Carey heard the door behind her creak open. A heavy but comforting arm rested on her shoulder. 'Hello, darling,' said Max. He turned her slightly to him and kissed her firmly on the lips. She almost fell against him with relief, making it seem as though she was enthusiastically returning the kiss. It wasn't too far from the truth.

'Have we got a visitor?' Max held out his hand. 'Hi, I'm Carey's fiancé. The one she fell hopelessly in love with, causing her to run off to deepest, darkest Cornwall. And you are?'

'This is Dean, darling.' The endearment fell easily from her lips. Max *was* a darling. 'The ex I told you about. I've just been trying to convince him how much in love we are.' She looked up at Max with loving eyes. It didn't take much acting, because at that moment she realized she'd gone past the 'falling in love' stage and was indeed hopelessly, helplessly in love with him.

Max kissed her nose. 'Who cares what others think? We know the truth, don't we, my love? Sorry . . . what was that name again? Dean? Yeah, sorry, Dean, but now I've got her, I'm never letting her go. We're going back to the States to have loads more babies.' Max patted her tummy, and his inference was clear. 'What can I say, Dean? I'm crazy about her. You know how that feels, don't you?'

'I won't let her go,' said Dean. 'Carey, you don't have to marry him just because you're pregnant. I'll take you and the baby if I have to.'

'I wasn't giving you an option,' said Max, stepping forward. Dean had no chance. Max was taller, more handsome, more intelligent and, Carey thought, more forceful. It was strange how such behaviour in him could seem so attractive to her, when the same behaviour in Dean was so sinister. 'As far as babies are concerned, I'm quite capable of taking responsibility for my own children, thank you very much. I'm telling you now that I intend for Carey to be Mrs. Winter, and neither you nor anyone else is going to stop me.'

'You don't love her as much as I do, Winter.'

'No, you're right,' said Max. 'I love her more. Now get off my property, and don't come back, because the next time I'll involve the police. Understood?'

Dean looked as if he might argue, but like all bullies he couldn't stand up to a stronger personality. He tried one last time to stare Max out and failed, so he got into his car and drove away at breakneck speed. The car backfired again, making Carey jump.

'Did you see it?' she asked, looking up at Max with wide, frightened eyes. 'Did you see what he was like?'

'Yes, I saw it. I was listening for a while. Come on inside and sit down.'

'I didn't hear you come back,' she said, a bit stupidly, as he led her to the lounge.

'I called at the stables first, so drove through the back way.'

'Oh. But you could see what I see in him? How unpleasant he is, I mean.'

'Sit down.' Max settled her on the

sofa. He made a call to the kitchen for a pot of tea. Then he came back and sat on a footstool in front of her. Carey had picked up a cushion and was hugging it to her chest. 'I saw it, Carey. You don't have to try and prove to me what he's like. If you want, I'll talk to your mom and try and make her see.'

Carey nodded as tears fell. 'Yes, please.'

Max smiled. 'Strange — I thought you were going to chew me up about having it all under control.'

'So did I, but as much as I'd have preferred to handle it myself, I'm glad you were there, Max. Thank you for what you did. It's a good job he hadn't met Jake, really. The only trouble is that when I go back home, he's going to realise it's not true and . . . '

'Don't worry about that for now. Stay here a few more days and then we can decide what you can do when you go home. You could stay at the hotel, but I think you'll be safer here in case he comes back. Sorry, I don't want to sound like him. As if I know what's best for you or like I'm trying to control what you do. But . . . '

'You don't. Honestly. You sound kind and thoughtful, and not at all like Jake's evil big brother of the legends. I'm grateful for that. But if I stay here I might get too used to you rescuing me.' She smiled a little but for her it was a serious subject. It wasn't the first time she'd thought how easy it would be to rely on Max. She had to remind herself that everything he'd said to Dean was a lie, whilst all the time wishing she could go off to America with him and have his babies. The thought made her blush so much, she hugged the cushion closer. 'I can't be the damsel in distress for the rest of my life. Besides, with all the problems I cause you, I'm sure I've outstayed my welcome.'

'Let me decide when I've had enough of rescuing you, and when you've outstayed your welcome.'

'Thanks for that, Max, but I have to sort it out for myself. Really I do. After all, you're not always going to be there. I need to do it for the sake of my own self-esteem. I hate feeling like some helpless little woman when he's around.' Or when Max was around for that matter, but she didn't say so.

'You feel how he wants you to feel,' said Max. Carey wondered if that was how he wanted her to feel, too. She didn't think so but she wasn't sure. His help seemed genuine, and she knew that if she insisted on walking out of there, he wouldn't stop her. *Because he doesn't love you*, a contrary little voice in her head whispered.

'But like I said,' Max added, 'let's not talk about that now. When you're feeling less rattled, we can work out what we're going to do about Dean. Ah, thanks, Sheila.'

The housekeeper entered the room with a tray of tea things and put them on the coffee table. 'Are you all right, Miss Ashmore? You look really rattled. Have a nice cuppa and it will calm you down.'

'I'm fine,' said Carey. 'And please stop calling me Miss Ashmore. It's Carey.'

'I'll sort that out, Sheila,' said Max. 'You go back to what you were doing.'

'Aye aye, Cap'n.' Sheila gave him a jaunty salute.

'She's a sweetheart,' said Carey when Sheila had gone.

'Yeah, she's okay.'

'She fancies you,' Carey said impishly.

Max raised an eyebrow and grinned wryly. 'And all this time I never knew what smouldering passion lay behind the kitchen door.' He became more serious. 'We need to talk, Carey. We have to get some things out into the open. Are you up to it?' He poured out a mug of tea and handed it to her.

'I'm not a china doll, Max. I'm fine. Just a bit shaken, that's all.'

'Okay, so tell me the real reason why you came here with Jake. I won't judge you or anything. I just need to know the truth.'

'We're not really engaged,' said Carey, relieved to have been asked a straight question. 'Despite whatever he told you this morning. He said you wouldn't let him have his trust fund until he was thirty. He said that you were deliberately withholding it. So he had this idea that if you thought he had settled down and was going to get married, you'd release his trust fund early. That was when he asked me to pretend to be his fiancée. He didn't pay me,' she added hastily, when she saw a strange look in Max's eyes. 'He just said I could have a week's holiday at the hotel, and after all the problems with Dean . . . I needed it.'

'His trust fund? That's what he told you this was all about?'

'Yes.'

Max laughed and it lit up his whole face. 'Carey, Jake received the money from his trust fund when he was twenty-one. He's had it, spent it, and come back for more since. That's all he really told you?'

'Yes. Why else would he ask me to pretend to be his fiancée?' Carey remembered what Ralph Wareham had said about the pretty, ordinary little girls that Jake brought home before. Was she really one of many? And if so, why?

'It's a long story. But the most important thing I want to know is, you're not engaged to Jake?'

She wondered why it was so important for him to know that. 'No.'

'And you're not in love with him?'

'No. Everything else we've told you is true, Max. We were at university together and we were friends, then he came to work at the centre after he was sacked from his last job. We're not a couple. I'm not in love with him, nor have I ever been.'

'Well that's a relief,' said Max.

8

Carey had no time to ask Max what he meant by his remark as the other house guests all began to emerge from their respective bedrooms. Had he meant that he was relieved she wasn't marrying into his family? Given the state of her confused emotions, it was the only explanation she could think of.

Rebecca and Tristan's father came to the lounge door and said curtly, 'Talk to you a minute, Max.'

Max nodded just as curtly and followed him out of the room. It left Carey with the three bridesmaids, the two mothers, Stephanie's father and Aunt Jane, none of whom had much to say to her, or to each other for that matter. It wasn't the friendliest of groups. Aunt Jane was clearly still hung over, and muttered something about the hair of the dog. 'Be a dear, will you,

Carey, and pour me a small gin and tonic.' Carey couldn't resist a look at the clock. It was only just after ten. 'Oh, ignore that,' said Aunt Jane. 'The sun will be over the yardarm somewhere in the world, I'm sure. You look as if you could do with a drink yourself, dear. Pour us one each then come and sit with me.'

So as not to seem unfriendly, Carey poured a gin and tonic for Aunt Jane ('When I said small, dear, I didn't mean you should just threaten the glass with the gin. Tip the bottle up a little further . . . a bit more. That's it. You're learning.') She poured a ginger ale for herself, feeling it looked suitably alcoholic. She sat on the sofa, but near to Aunt Jane's chair.

'I think we might head off home,' said Stephanie's father. 'Tell Max we said goodbye.' Carey couldn't help thinking it was a bit ungrateful not to thank their host personally for having them.

The three bridesmaids decided to

leave too, talking of stopping off in town for some shopping and lunch. Mrs. Pilkington waited a few minutes, and then went in search of her husband.

'Was it something we said, do you think?' asked Aunt Jane.

'This is such a strange house,' said Carey to no one in particular. She sipped her ginger ale.

'We're a strange family. Have Jake and Rebecca run off together yet?'

Carey nodded. 'Yes, I rather think so. Max has taken it well.'

'Tsk,' said Aunt Jane, taking a large slug from her drink. 'Ah, that's better. You've made the mistake of believing what she wanted Jake to believe. She isn't Max's girlfriend. I don't even think he likes her very much. Not surprising really, given the problems that girl and Jake have caused in this family.'

'What do you mean?'

'So you don't know about it all then?'

'Nope. I'm clueless.'

'Sit back and let me tell you the story. You look as if you're ready to jump up and leave at any minute.'

'Perhaps it would be best if I did.' Nevertheless, Carey did as she was bid, half-turning to face Aunt Jane and resting her chin on her hand.

'Jake and Rebecca have known each other since they were children,' said Aunt Jane. 'No one in either family would have minded if they grew up to get married, and most of us expected it, but they're a strange pair. Not quite right in the head, if you ask me.' Aunt Jane tapped her temple to illustrate. 'They wanted drama and excitement, and to believe they're star-crossed lovers. They like the thrill of their love being illicit. So from the very beginning they've played with each other's — and sadly, other people's — emotions. Rebecca went off and married Ralph Wareham just to hurt Jake. Then Jake wasn't happy until he'd won her back from Ralph, destroying that marriage in the process. They managed about a fortnight together before Jake ran off with some waitress he met in a night club. Rebecca won him back from her. And so it goes on . . . and on . . . and on. You're not the first young lady Jake has brought here to make Rebecca jealous. I doubt you'll be the last. So now they've run off together again, and it will last a week or so — no more than a month — until they get bored with the day-to-day fact of living together. Then they'll have to do something else to destroy each other. Either Rebecca will up and marry someone, or Jake will. Or they'll just run off with someone else. Meanwhile, others will get hurt. It destroyed Ralph Wareham. And a few nice girls like yourself.'

'I can assure you, I'm not hurt by Jake's behaviour, Aunt Jane. But it's all so ludicrous. No one behaves like that, surely?'

'Jake and Rebecca do. You noticed the freezing temperatures between the families, of course. Jake's family blames Rebecca. Rebecca's family blames Jake.

Only Max, and perhaps myself, see it like it really is. I'm not joking when I say they're sick, Carey. One day the thrill of being illicit will bore them, and maybe then they'll up the stakes. They'll end up doing something far more serious.'

'You think they might do physical damage to each other?'

Aunt Jane nodded. 'Oh, I know you think I'm a drunken old woman, and probably talking through the bottom of a glass, but I'm telling the truth as I see it.'

'I must admit I can't imagine Jake having such passionate feelings. He's so laid-back, he's almost horizontal.'

'Yes, he probably is nowadays. That wasn't always the case. It's all an act now. A facsimile of feelings they had as teenagers, and a desperate and rather pathetic attempt to keep it all going. The passion, the excitement, the hurt. Rebecca won't always be beautiful, and Jake won't always be good-looking. So their ability to attract others in the future will diminish. That's when I think things will turn really sour. I blame films and books.'

'Why?' Carey frowned.

'Because the passions in them are always so heightened, dear. People fall in love in an instant, and go to bed together just as quickly, and those who read the books or watch the films want love to be the same. An overwhelming compulsion, where Leonardo Di Caprio is willing to die for a girl he spent all of one night with — and in the back of a car at that . . . *Titanic* isn't nearly as classy as they make out. But most of the time, in real life, young lovers are forcing the emotions to prosper instead of waiting for love to grow naturally. Oh listen to me. Perhaps I have had too much to drink.' Carey was put in mind of the old adage of a drunken woman speaking sober words. Aunt Jane talked more sense than anyone else she'd met that weekend, apart from Max.

'I think it's possible to fall in love with someone very quickly,' said Carey, looking into her own glass.

'That's because you weren't looking for it, dear,' said Aunt Jane kindly. 'So there's nothing forced about the way you feel.' Carey's head snapped up and she saw Aunt Jane looking at her with shrewd eyes. The old lady reached over and patted her shoulder. 'Bless you. It's been obvious since you entered this room at dinner on Friday.'

'What's been obvious?' Neither of them had noticed Max entering the room.

'That Carey is far too good for Jake,' said Aunt Jane. 'I've just been filling her in on the saga.'

'Good. It'll save me the trouble.' Max slumped down on the sofa, looking suddenly very tired. 'I've just had Pilkington-Smythe giving me what-for, wanting to know why I don't control Jake better. I suggested he try the same with his daughter; that way he'd know exactly how easy it is to tell a grown-up in their mid-twenties what to do. Though I use the term 'grown-up' loosely where both Jake and Rebecca are concerned.'

For the first time since she'd arrived, Carey felt that the air at Manishi was clear. All the secrets were out, the tension caused by Jake, Rebecca and the relatives had evaporated, and all they had left was honesty and companionship between the three of them. It made her feel more relaxed than she had been when she arrived. Max looked around as if he had just realised the same. 'Have all the other rats deserted the ship?'

'They have,' said Jane.

'Then why don't I take you two ladies into Newquay for lunch? Or maybe up to Tintagel. We'll show Carey the castle.'

'I'm going to rest this afternoon, if that's all right with you, Max,' said Jane. 'I'll be heading home tonight.'

'You don't have to leave yet, Jane. You're my favourite guest.'

'But something of a gooseberry at the moment. Go on, the pair of you. Off to

Tintagel and lunch. Say hello to King Arthur for me.'

'You look tired, Max,' Carey said. 'Don't feel you have to entertain me. Why don't you just relax for the day?'

'I'm not planning on running a marathon through Cornwall.' He smiled. 'It will be relaxing to be with you.' His voice had a gently caressing tone to it.

'So,' said Max as they drove north towards Tintagel about an hour later. 'Now you know the truth about Jake and Rebecca.' It was a gorgeous day, without a cloud in the sky. Carey just sat back and enjoyed the scenery and Max's company. Once she returned home she might never see him again, so she decided to make the most of it. She still didn't know why he was so relieved about her not loving Jake, but she tried not to think about it. He'd always been kind to her, despite his reputation as an evil Big Brother, and he didn't seem like a snob. But one never knew.

'Yes, though it all seems unbelievable.

Not that I doubt Aunt Jane's word. It's like you suggested, grown-ups don't behave that way. Then again, grown-ups accept when a relationship is over. Did you really think I was in on it?'

'Well you clearly weren't in love with Jake, so that left me with two options. You were in on it, or . . . it doesn't matter now.'

'What? After his money?'

Max nodded slightly. 'Maybe. I don't know, Carey. I have to admit it seems at odds with you. You seem too honest. Even when you were lying, you hated it. I could tell. You were like a frightened kitten on Friday night.'

'I'm no angel, Max, but I do try to be honest with people. I knew his plot had more holes than a leaky boat!'

Max threw back his head and laughed. 'You have a way of putting things that no one else does. Do you know that?'

'I have been told. But I'm going to have to be more sensible. I've come to the conclusion that if I didn't have such an over-active imagination, then Mum might have believed me where Dean is concerned.'

'That's not your fault. He knew the right things to say to her. Every mom likes to think their daughter is going to be looked after by the man in her life.'

Carey shivered and hugged herself, as if thinking of Dean had made the sun go in. 'Let's not talk about him. Let's just have a nice afternoon.'

'I agree.'

'But I'm buying lunch.'

'I don't agree.'

'Max . . . I'm going to have to try and teach you a bit about taking instead of giving before I go home.'

'Do you know, if you had a drink in your hand right now you'd look and sound just like Aunt Jane?'

'Do you know that if you weren't driving and didn't therefore have my life in your hands, I'd have to slap your wrists for that?'

9

Tintagel is a small town with winding roads and quaint old cottages. It has links with King Arthur, on account of the castle being where King Arthur was allegedly conceived. The local populace naturally cashes in on that for the tourism trade. Every other shop or café is named for some Arthurian legend.

Carey and Max spent a leisurely couple of hours visiting the castle, which is set out on a rocky peninsula, and the Old Post Office — a medieval building which is cared for by the National Trust — before browsing the gift shops on the main street. They then found a little café which served up an authentic Welsh rarebit. Cornwall was a couple of hours from Wales, but the Arthurian legends stretched there, too, as did many other Celtic myths.

'What is Welsh rarebit?' asked Max

when they'd ordered.

'The best comfort food in the world ever,' said Carey. 'My mum's Welsh and she used to make it for me when I was poorly as a child.'

'Are there any particular traditions I should remember? I don't want to make a fool of myself like I did in the fish restaurant yesterday.'

'Now you're teasing me,' said Carey.

'I know. It's deliberate, just so I can get a look at those adorable dimples of yours.'

She rewarded him with a show of them. 'I can't believe how little of Cornwall you've actually seen since you moved here,' she said.

'I guess I've been busy rebuilding the house, then working at the company. Besides, I've had no one to go with.'

'I find that hard to believe. There must be lots of women in Cornwall who'd enjoy spending a day with you.'

'I guess I haven't had much time for that either. And . . . '

'What?'

'I haven't really been looking. I guess Mom and Dad's divorce soured me against relationships, so I've tended to keep women at arm's length. I don't want to make the mistake my folks did.'

'Taking someone out on a date doesn't imply certain marriage.'

'I know that, but you'd be surprised how many women think of it first when they find out I've got money. I don't much figure as a person.'

'I can't decide if you're being too hard on them or on yourself, Max. You're a nice man.'

'That sounds boring.'

'No, it isn't! Do you know, I thought Rebecca was your girlfriend. All that stuff about her leaving her clothes at your house and . . . It's probably none of my business anyway.' Carey had forgotten what Rebecca had said about her dress and the opera until that moment. Somehow it made her uncertain again.

'I'll give you an explanation if you want.'

'Like I said, it's none of my business. And we've been saved by the food again. Thank you.'

The waitress brought their Welsh rarebit and set it in front of them. They ate in silence for a while, with Carey feeling that she'd intruded where she didn't belong.

'She stayed overnight with Tristan for one of the many wedding rehearsals,' said Max after a few minutes. 'And she definitely had her own room.'

Carey had trouble swallowing her food, but once she managed it she just said, 'Oh.'

'There have been other women in my life, Carey,' Max continued. 'But I promise you that Rebecca isn't one of them.'

'It doesn't really matter anyway,' she said, trying to sound casual. 'Not to me. I mean, it's just that . . . well the stuff with Jake. I saw them together at the Italian restaurant, you see, and I thought she was cheating on you. So I'm just relieved for your sake that she wasn't.'

'So that's why we had to have fish and chips instead of Italian. It was kind of you to try and spare me the pain, but completely unnecessary.'

'Well I know that now!'

'Strange — I felt the same when I saw them meeting up on the balcony the night before. I didn't want you to be hurt.'

Carey laughed. 'It's like a book or film, isn't it? If only people would just ask the right questions or say what they really mean, all the misunderstandings might be sorted out quickly. It's funny but the first time I read *Rebecca*, I wondered why on earth the second Mrs. de Winter didn't just stick up for herself. I couldn't imagine not doing so in a similar situation. Now I understand better how hard it is to say what you think. It took me a long time to pluck up the courage to tell Dean it was over. And it wouldn't make for much of a story, I suppose.'

'I thought there might be another reason you were concerned,' said Max, frowning a little at her mention of Dean. 'About me and the real Rebecca, I mean.'

'No, no. Like I said, none of my business.' She didn't want to admit that even the idea of them being a couple still sent a sharp pain piercing through her.

'It looks like this story is going to run for a while longer.'

'What do you mean?' She looked across at him. His eyes were twinkling mischievously. He looked devastatingly handsome and far too magnificent for the little tea room. He was probably far too magnificent for her too, she thought with a sinking heart.

'I don't think I'll answer that, because we clearly haven't reached the denouement yet, despite having sorted out the misunderstanding about Jake and Rebecca, and managing to dispense with Dean. I guess there's another act to go that we don't know about.'

'Did that waitress slip something alcoholic into your Welsh rarebit? I've only got Worcester sauce on mine. Maybe she gave you brandy.'

'Gee thanks. I try to contribute some imagination and magic to our story, along with a little more dramatic tension, and you question my sobriety.'

Something about the way he said 'our story' made Carey thrill, but she kept up the light bantering tone, afraid of spoiling the mood. 'You hit your head in the castle. That's it, isn't it? Because you're so tall and the ceilings are so low. I imagine King Arthur was only about four feet tall. And most of the knights, for that matter. I bet giants in those days were only about five-foot ten.'

'I'm deeply hurt. My storytelling skills are obviously wasted on you.'

'Not wasted. I'm just disappointed. You're an American, for goodness sake. Shouldn't there be lots of explosions and Bruce Willis running around in a vest?'

'I'm saving the fireworks for last. As for Bruce, there's no way he's getting the girl this time. Now eat your grilled cheese.'

'Welsh rarebit.'

'That's a fancy name for a plate of grilled cheese. With a poached egg.'

'Philistine.'

They carried on in that vein, earning amused looks from the other diners and the two middle-aged waitresses.

'What now?' asked Max when they'd finished eating and Carey had insisted on paying for the food.

'Don't you have to get back?'

'Not particularly. Would you like to drive along the coast, down to Land's End?'

'Isn't that a long way?'

'A couple of hours. We could have dinner there. Then it's about an hour back to Manishi. It'll be a great drive in this weather.'

'Okay, yes. It sounds lovely.' She didn't want the day to end. She couldn't remember ever enjoying anyone's company as much. Why she'd ever thought of Max as scary, she didn't know, though it probably had much to do with Jake's tall tales about his brother. Max made her feel safe and happy. And even if it was dangerous to feel that way, and there was a possibility of her heart being torn in two, she intended to cherish the short time she had with him. That way, on cold winter nights she'd be able to look back and remember these moments. 'Go and wait in the car for me. I want to go back to the gift shop in the castle.'

'Why?'

'That would be telling.'

'Carey, you don't have to . . . '

'I want to.'

Before Max could argue, Carey was out of the door and halfway to the castle, where she made her purchases.

There were several car parks in Tintagel. Max had parked his car in one on Atlantic Road, so Carey made her way back there. She heard her mobile phone ring and stopped momentarily to answer it. Just as she saw the call came from Max, she felt a hand grab her arm and manfully push her towards a car which in her shock she didn't immediately recognize. Everything was a blur. She felt a sharp object in her back.

'Do as you're told, Carey and I won't hurt you.'

'Dean? For God's sake . . . '

'Get into the back seat.'

Terrified, she did as she was told. Dean got into the driver's seat. 'The doors have child locks,' he told her. 'So you can't get out. You're coming home with me.' He started the car, which immediately backfired. Carey jumped involuntarily, as if he'd fired a gun at her.

She couldn't believe what was happening. They were on a busy street in the middle of a bustling tourist centre and she was being kidnapped. Such things didn't happen in real life. Her phone was still ringing. She looked down at her bag, which she still clutched, along with the carrier bag from the gift shop.

'Don't answer it,' said Dean. She didn't know if he was armed or not. She vaguely remembered feeling something sharp against her back as he pushed her into the car, but his hands on the steering wheel were empty.

Questions ran through Carey's head, like why had Aunt Jane not warned them sooner? Unless she'd tried to. Mobile phone signals in the area were hit and miss, plus there was so much noise from tourists it was sometimes hard to hear the phone when it did ring. And if she were honest, neither she nor Max was listening for it, being so wrapped up with the enjoyment of the day. Her heart gave a pang. What if they were the last moments she'd ever spend with him? What if this was it? The end of her life. She struggled to keep calm. If she became hysterical then it might force Dean into behaving rashly. She suppressed a sudden burst of laughter. Rashly? He couldn't have behaved less rashly if he'd tried.

'Do you really think threatening me

with a weapon is going to make me suddenly fall in love with you?' she asked Dean, trying hard to keep the tremor out of her voice. Everything depended on her keeping her head and looking for any means of escape.

'It's a bit extreme, I admit. But I had to get your attention.' His hands trembled on the wheel. 'Good old Aunt Jane told me the truth about you and the Winter bloke. You're not engaged to him or his brother! So I can only assume you've done all this to make me jealous.'

'If you've hurt her, Dean . . . '

'Hurt her? She was so drunk that she didn't even remember meeting me yesterday. I didn't have to force her to tell me a thing. She blurted it all out. And then fell asleep before I left.'

Carey wondered where Sheila was whilst all this was happening. Had she gone home? If Max hadn't been calling Carey about Dean then he might not even know Dean was in Tintagel. He may have just been calling to see where she was. She had to hope he would wonder where she'd gone eventually. Given her lack of fuss — or so it seemed to her — over getting into the car, Max might believe she'd gone willingly and assume she'd decided to go back to her ex. Then he'd just go back to Manishi and forget about her. She knew that would happen one day anyway, but it still hurt to think of it.

'So what's the plan, Dean? Are you going to have a shotgun in my back all the way up the aisle? Hmm?'

'Carey, it won't be like that once we've got away and had time to ourselves. You'll see then that this thing you've got for Max Winter is just an aberration. I can see why you were attracted to him. He's got those movie-star good looks. And he's rich.' Carey went to protest but thought better of it. Dean would never understand. He would only believe what he wanted to believe. 'But it's me you love.'

He'd taken the road north from

Tintagel. As far as Carey remembered, it joined the A39 somewhere along the route. But that didn't lead to home; it just skirted the coastline of Cornwall. It was just what she should have been doing with Max, but in the opposite direction. She couldn't think about that. It hurt too much. *Please let him miss me a little*, she prayed silently.

'Dean, you can't force me to love you by kidnapping me at knife-point. What does that say about the rest of our lives together? That you're going to threaten to harm me every time I do something you don't like?'

'It won't be like that. Once we're married, we'll both feel more secure.'

'No, I don't think you will. I think you'll get sicker and sicker until you do something awful.' She was thinking of what Aunt Jane had said about Jake and Rebecca. Only now did she realize that it also applied to Dean. 'And I'm not about to take that risk. So drag me back home if you like. But I am never going to be your wife.'

'You're tired, darling. Why don't you get some sleep?'

His intransigence was frightening and very annoying. 'Oh I'm sick of this.' Carey glanced down and saw the carrier bag. If Dean, like Jake and Rebecca, craved drama, she'd give it to him. It was a long shot, but it might just work. It might also make him crash the car either accidentally or on purpose, but that was a chance she had to take.

She felt around the bag to make sure of her bearings, then as he concentrated on the road she suddenly pushed one of the objects inside into a point and pressed it to the space between his shoulders. 'You're not the only one with a weapon, Dean. This is a mini ceremonial sword that I bought as a present for Max. But it has a very real blade. Now, you're going to turn this car around and take me right back to him. Because, whether you believe it or not, I love him, and I will love him for the rest of my life in a way I can never love you.' She struggled to keep her voice calm on the last few words.

'Carey . . . ' Dean faltered. 'Now don't be stupid.'

'There's a roundabout up ahead. Go all the way around it and back down this road. I'm warning you, Dean.'

He glanced at her through the rear-view mirror. His eyes startled. But he did as she asked. 'Carey . . . '

'Don't talk to me anymore. I don't want to listen to anything you have to say. After you've dropped me back off with Max, you'll go away from me and never bother me or my family again. If you can't make that promise, then I'll contact the police as soon as we get back into Tintagel.' She was tempted to take her phone out there and then to prove her point, but was afraid of losing the upper hand by fumbling to dial a number.

'I know we're meant to be together, Carey.'

'No we're not.' She jabbed him in the back to illustrate her point. 'Love affairs end, Dean. It's sad when it happens, but it's a fact of life. You can't force someone to love you. You have to move on and hope that you find someone else who will love you. That's how normal people do it.'

'I love you.'

'No you don't. Because if you loved me, you'd want the best for me. You'd want me to be happy, even if I don't include you in my life.' She was thinking of Max as she spoke, knowing that as hard as it might seem, she would walk away from him. Assuming she ever saw him again to be able to walk away. 'What you want is to control and possess me, and I'm not going to let that happen. I've let you have too much power over me as it is. Well no more. The next time you come knocking on my door or bothering the people I love, I'll call the police.' She jabbed a bit harder. 'And you definitely keep away from my mother!' They were back in Tintagel. 'That car park, down there on the left.'

To Carey's dismay, she couldn't see

Max's car. Had he assumed she'd gone? Dean pulled into a parking bay and was about to turn around and grab Carey's arm.

'Don't even think about it.'

Dean moved slightly and a knife fell from his lap to the floor at his feet. Carey shuddered involuntarily.

The next bit would be a problem. He said the child locks were on all the other doors, so how could she get out? Her heart beat rapidly. She was still as trapped as she'd been when they were driving along the road. She need not have worried. Seconds later, Dean's door was yanked open and a familiar muscular arm dragged him out of the car.

By the time Carey opened the window and managed to unlock her side, Dean was lying flat on his back, with Max towering over him. 'I swear to God if you've hurt her . . . ' Max was saying, his hand held back ready to punch Dean in the face. A policeman was at Max's side, pulling him back.

'That's quite enough, Mr. Winter. Let us deal with this. I don't want to have to arrest you, too. Now.' The policeman looked down at Dean. 'Would you mind telling us why you abducted the young lady, sir?'

'He had a knife,' said Carey. She pointed to the front of the car. A female PC stepped forward and quickly put on some latex gloves, picking it up. 'I haven't handled it,' Carey explained. 'I've seen *CSI*. So the fingerprints and DNA should be intact.'

Max grinned and said to the policewoman, 'That little quirk of hers is adorable when you get to know her.' The policewoman looked as though she would take his word for it, but was also gazing at him with obvious admiration. Handsome six-foot-plus Americans were few and far between in Cornwall, and Max was a particularly fine example.

'I wasn't going to use it,' said Dean. 'Besides, she's got a knife. She threatened me with it.' He was rubbing his jaw, and Carey guessed that a bruise would soon start showing. She glanced at Max with loving eyes. She abhorred violence of any kind. Of course she did. There was absolutely no excuse for it. But she couldn't help feeling a little pleased that Max had turned into a real-life action hero, and for her sake. Who needed Bruce Willis and his vest anyway?

'Have you got a knife, Ms. Ashmore?' asked the policewoman. Carey got the impression that as a rival for Max's affections, the WPC would have liked an excuse to lock her up.

'No, not at all. I've only got this.' She pulled a small sword and a shield from the carrier bag. It was nothing more than a child's toy. 'It's only plastic, though that tip is a bit lethal. I admit I let him think it was a knife, to make him turn around. It was self-defence. I'm sure any court would agree.'

'I wondered why he went all the way around the roundabout,' said Max with a grin.

'You saw that?'

'I heard his car backfire in the distance and guessed what had happened. I was behind you all the way.'

'You were?' Carey smiled. Then because she couldn't help herself, she flew into Max's arms and kissed him. 'My hero . . . '

10

'What will you be doing when you go back to work?' asked Aunt Jane over dinner. She had sobered up quickly after being told what Dean had done to Carey. It was hard for either Max or Carey to be angry with her in the face of her contrition. She vowed never to touch another drop, then promptly asked for a gin and tonic. ('My nerves are shattered, Max dear.')

'We're studying *The Picture of Dorian Grey*,' said Carey, picking at her plate of pasta. She was feeling awkward again, especially after kissing Max so openly. They hadn't had much chance to talk since. Dean had been arrested and was due to appear in the local magistrates' court in the morning. Carey told the police that she was content to take out a restraining order, since he hadn't done her any real harm.

She hoped it was the right thing to do. A warning shot might stop him from acting the same with any other girl. Even if he was charged with abducting her, she doubted he would get a prison term. Not for a first offence. But by the time they saw him off with the police, he seemed to have accepted that it was really over between him and Carey. 'She's bloody mental,' he had told the policewoman.

'Oh no,' Max was saying in resigned but amused tones. 'Do I have to take you up to the attic and prove to you there's no portrait depicting all my sins, whilst I remain young and beautiful? Or is it enough for me to promise you there isn't one?'

'Yes there is, dear,' said Aunt Jane. 'It's behind mine.' They all laughed, breaking the tension that had existed since their return home.

Later that night, after Aunt Jane had gone to bed, Carey and Max sat in the lounge having a quiet drink. There was so much she wanted to say to him, but she felt shy, like a sixteen-year-old at her first party.

'You never told me why you bought the toy sword and shield,' said Max.

'Oh, I forgot all about it with all those dramatics.' She'd left the bag up in her room. 'I bought it for you, so you can rescue damsels in distress, or maidens tied to railway lines. That sort of thing.'

'You were the one who took down a man with a plastic sword,' he said with a smile that suggested he was proud of her. Then he added a little ruefully, 'You hardly needed me to rescue you.'

She fought the instinct to fly across the room into his arms and tell him just how desperately she did need him. Not as a helpless damsel, but as a woman, and in the hope that he needed her just as much. The fear of rejection silenced her. Hadn't he said it was a relief she wasn't marrying Jake? If he didn't want her to be in his brother's life, it was unlikely he'd want her to be in his.

'I'm sure there are lots more damsels out there in need of protection,' she said.

Max frowned. 'If you don't end this story soon, it will be up to me to do it, and I'm not as good at this as you are. Only . . . '

'What?'

'You've been through a lot. Not just today but with Dean in the past few months. Maybe it would be wrong of me to ask any more from you for now. Let's get some rest, then tomorrow we'll attempt the trip down to Land's End again. It might be a fitting place to bring the story to a close.'

Carey felt deflated. The only ending she could see to the story was her returning to Derbyshire and never seeing Max again. 'I think . . . you've been really kind . . . but I should go home tomorrow. I suppose the story ends with me riding off into the sunset. But on a train, rather than a horse. I'm not very good with horses, as you know.'

'That depends if you're alone or not.' It seemed like they were playing a game with each other, and Carey was put in mind of the games Jake and Rebecca played. Was the suggestive tone in Max's voice part of that game? A way of playing with her affections?

'Of course I'll be alone. You don't think I want Dean back, do you? And as for Jake . . . ' When she saw his exasperated expression, and realised that once again she'd misunderstood him, she twisted her fingers together. 'Max, please don't play those games with me. I'm not sophisticated enough to deal with them.'

'You're not sophisticated at all.' It felt as though he'd crushed her, even though he'd said it kindly enough and with a smile that bordered on affectionate. 'What I mean is . . . '

She jumped up from the sofa. 'Never mind. I'm exhausted and it's time I went to bed. Good night.' Before he could reply she was out of the room and halfway up the stairs.

* * *

Carey was trapped in the back of Dean's car. She frantically tried the doors, but they were locked. Dean was both driving the car and sitting in the back seat with her. She didn't think to question this anomaly, only trembling at the thought of him being everywhere. She glanced out of the window and saw Max. Her heart flipped. He was carrying the plastic sword and shield. He'd soon save her. Instead he climbed onto a horse, which suddenly appeared out of nowhere, and rode off towards the sunset, which was odd as she was sure it was still the middle of the day. He was going to rescue some other girl, because she'd been too scared to tell him how she really felt. It served her right to be stuck with Dean. But she had to try and stop Max from going.

'Max!' she cried. 'Max, don't leave me with him. Max! Max!'

'It's all right, darling. I'm here.' Now it was dark and he was holding her closely. Carey opened her eyes. A sob escaped from her throat.

'You left me . . . ' That strange land between sleep and wakefulness evaporated, and she really was awake, lying in her bed. Max had lain down next to her and was cradling her in his arms, stroking her hair and covering her brow with tender kisses. 'No, I didn't leave you.'

She snuggled in closer to him, revelling in his male aroma and the strength of his body. 'Will you stay with me, please?'

'Of course I will.' He pulled her closer still. 'We'll chase those nightmares away together, hmm?'

Carey must have dozed a little, because when she woke up he was under the covers with her and they were lying in a spoons position. She shifted her body a little so that she was almost moulded to his, luxuriating in the closeness and the sensuality he evoked in her. Her fingers traced the line of his bare arm, which was wrapped around her waist. She thought he was sleeping until his hand moved, gently caressing her belly, the heat searing through her nightshirt. His mouth teased the nape of her neck, sending tiny explosions coursing through her body. 'Max . . . ' she whispered, turning to face him.

'Are you sure you want this, darling?' She loved him even more for taking the time to ask properly instead of taking her acceptance for granted.

'I've never wanted anything more in my whole life.' As he enveloped her in his arms, and his lips found hers, she made a silent vow that whatever else happened in her life, and even if he sent her away the next day, she would never forget Max Winter.

He took her gently — so gently that at one point she whispered, 'You won't break me, Max.' That appeared to be all he needed to know. Gentle strokes became wild thrusts. Carey forgot that Aunt Jane was down the hall. She forgot all the fear and pain of her dream and just gave herself up to him wholeheartedly.

She didn't regret being with him that night. Her only regret in the cold light of day was that such a wonderful experience might never happen again.

He didn't send her home, and when they woke up he treated her with great tenderness and respect. But he hadn't made any grand declarations of love or asked her to stay with him forever. Well, she chided herself, what did she expect when they'd only known each other a few days? Her own feelings were out of control, though she tried hard to hide them so as not to frighten him off. Who knew where their relationship would go? It was far too early to say and it would be wrong of her to force things. Just as wrong as Dean trying to force her to love him.

'Shall we try for Land's End again today?' he asked over breakfast.

'Yes, that would be lovely.'

'I have to drive Aunt Jane home first, but we'll go later.'

'I could come with you. To take Aunt Jane, I mean.'

'Er . . . sorry, darling, I have some business to take care of. Will you be okay here on your own? Or we could drop you off in Newquay.'

'I'll stay here,' Carey said breezily, trying to hide her disappointment that he didn't seem to want to spend time with her. Perhaps it was his way of letting her down gently. 'I could do with a rest . . . I mean after the last few days . . . ' She blushed, realizing the implications of what she'd said in light of the night they'd just spent together. How could she still feel so shy with him?

'Perhaps we could both get some rest later, when Aunt Jane is safely at home.' The intimate promise in his voice lightened her heart a little. He wasn't ready to throw her out yet, which was something.

'I'd like that.'

He stood up and leaned across the table to kiss her. 'I'll go and wake Aunt

Jane, otherwise she'll stay in bed all day. Don't let any old hags lure you away with promises of shiny apples.' What he really meant was to take care if Dean returned, but she was glad he made a joke of it. She doubted they'd see Dean again, but for a moment she did worry.

So as not to let Max worry too, she quipped, 'You're rather tall for one of the seven dwarves. Which one are you?'

'Sleepy at the moment,' he said, winking. Carey blushed scarlet. 'Or Happy. Probably a bit of both.'

She rewarded him with her widest smile. 'Yes, me too.'

'You're far too pretty to be any of the dwarves.'

'I'm hardly Snow White either.'

'For which I'm extremely grateful.'

'Will you go away and stop distracting me from my croissant?' What she really wanted to say was that he was welcome to make her happy and sleepy anytime he wanted.

Carey spent the morning alone, trying hard not to count the minutes until Max returned. Perhaps, she thought, she ought to just go and save him the embarrassment of having to pretend he'd call her. She felt angry with Dean. Not just because of the way he'd treated her, but also because of the way he'd forced her to think of the consequences of her own feelings for Max. She was afraid to tell Max that she loved him; afraid to ask him if they had a future, in case her love was unwanted. How would she react to that rejection? She hoped she'd do the decent thing and leave with her dignity intact. That was what she'd told Dean she would do and what she believed Dean should have done. But things had changed with Max. Now she wasn't entirely sure she wouldn't make a complete fool of herself by getting down on her knees and begging him to love her.

'No, you idiot,' she told her reflection in the bedroom mirror as she dressed for their afternoon out. 'You won't do that. You've got more pride than Dean.'

If only Max had given some indication, whilst they were alone together, that he cared just as much for her. Even if he had, she knew that she'd doubt any declarations of love made by a man during intimate moments. 'Why does love have to be so complicated?' she asked her reflection. It didn't have any more answers than she did. It did make her wonder why people like Jake, Rebecca and Dean went out of their way to make things even more complex. Surely there was a simpler way of loving someone.

She still meant to keep her promise about not regretting him. If she had to go, she might cry a little, and spend some time with a broken heart. But she would survive. And perhaps, though it seemed unlikely to her at that moment, she'd be able to fall in love again.

She ate lunch in the kitchen with Sheila, listening as the housekeeper nattered away about her children, adding some juicy gossip about the neighbours. 'I'll miss this place,' she said.

'Why? I didn't realize you were leaving,' said Carey.

'I'm not. Well not leaving Cornwall, but Max is. He told me last night that he's putting Manishi up for sale and moving back to America. I can't really blame him. He doesn't owe this family anything, despite what his father is meant to have said or not said on his death bed. They treat him like a bank, the lot of them.'

'Oh . . . ' Carey didn't know what to say. Part of her felt annoyed with Max for not telling her. But why should he? They weren't officially a couple. He didn't have to tell her anything about his plans. *I don't regret a thing, I don't regret a thing*, she affirmed inwardly. But would she have been so willing to spend the night with him if she'd known he was moving back to America? It would have been nice to have that choice.

When Max returned late in the afternoon, Carey had to work even harder to pretend nothing was wrong.

Not only did he not owe Jake's family anything, but he didn't owe her anything either.

'Are you ready?' he asked.

'Yes, but don't you want something to eat first?'

'Er . . . I'm not very hungry.' He seemed nervous about something. She guessed then that he was waiting till they got to Land's End to tell her of his plans, perhaps wanting to sugar the pill with some nice scenery. She braced herself, knowing it would hurt just as much wherever he told her, but also knowing that she wouldn't be begging him to love her no matter what her earlier fears were. As painful as it was, she had to let him go. To do otherwise would be to treat him as badly as Jake's family had, and she would never do that.

'We're taking a horse?' When Carey got outside, it was to find a horse box attached to the back of Max's car.

'Yeah . . . just some whim . . . '

She was tempted to ask him if he

intended to ride all the way back to America, but wasn't sure if she was supposed to know about it.

The easy atmosphere of the morning had altered. They both sat in silence as he drove south, and only exchanged small talk when they walked around Land's End. He left the horse at a local stable, where he appeared to know the owners. It occurred to her then that perhaps he was selling off his horses ready for the move.

They had dinner at a local restaurant. Carey thought she would explode with the tension building up inside her. She appreciated he was trying to make things nice for her, to soften the blow, but she really wished he would just get on with it.

When they left the restaurant, he took her hand and it was all she could do not to cry. He led her back towards the entrance to Land's End, and to her amazement, his friend was waiting there with the horse. Max thanked him before climbing onto the horse and, without a word, pulling Carey up behind him. She wrapped her arms around his waist and rested her head against his shoulder, hoping that he wouldn't feel her tears through his clothes. Then he started riding towards Land's End.

'Can you take horses in there?' she asked, just for something to say.

'You can if you make a sizeable donation to the organization that runs it,' he replied. He rode further on, towards the signpost that pointed to all directions of the globe, then came to a stop. The sun had begun to set, casting a golden glow over the coast. 'Where to now, Carey?' he asked. 'Do we keep on riding into that sunset, or just go back to the lives we had before?'

'I . . . er . . . Sheila told me you were going back to America, so I suppose . . .' Her voice broke. 'I suppose you'll be going one way and I'll be going another. Though I'm amazed you'd just leave . . . leave Manishi behind.'

'I was hoping to take my heart's

desire with me.'

'Yes, you could have it shipped over brick by brick,' she said. She'd heard of Americans doing that with English buildings.

'It's just a house, Carey. But I can't say it's one I've ever been happy in.' He climbed off the horse and pulled her down after him. 'What I meant was that I . . . oh . . . I've been rehearsing this all day and none of it is coming out the way I want it to. I can't stay in England. I've had enough of it here. Enough of that family. Not Jake — he's my brother, when all's said and done. And maybe not Aunt Jane. She's okay. But I'm done with the rest of them. I decided weeks ago that I'd go home once the wedding was over, and you turning up made it much more difficult for me. It could also be easy, if you give me the answer I want.' He ran his fingers through his hair. 'I'm afraid I'm pushing you into something you're not ready for. But I can't bear to go back home without you. I know it's a lot to ask, for you to give up your life in England, but the truth is I love you. I've loved you since the day you arrived . . . '

'Yes.'

'What?'

'Yes.' Suddenly love wasn't so complicated anymore. It was incredibly, wonderfully easy. 'Oh Max, I'll go anywhere with you. I love you too.'

He pulled her into his arms and they kissed as the sun set behind them. 'But,' said Carey, pulling away reluctantly, 'You said I wasn't sophisticated, and I worry . . . '

'Darling,' he said as he held her tightly, 'believe me when I say that was a compliment, not an insult. I love how — '

'Simple I am?'

'Far from it. I love how uncomplicated you are. How you don't play games, and you say exactly what you're thinking, even when you don't mean to.'

'You wouldn't say that if you knew

what I've been bottling up all day. Only I wasn't sure how you felt, and then last night you didn't say anything . . . '

'I wanted to, but I wanted you to be sure of my feelings, which is why I've waited until now. I love you, Carey Ashmore.' He paused. 'Would it really be so awful for you to be the future Mrs. Winter? I promise to remember your first name for the rest of our lives.'

'I'm quite happy to be Mrs. Winter forever.' She kissed him.

He lifted her up in his arms and spun her round. 'We did it. It took some doing, but we got to the end of the story.'

'I'm hoping this is only the end of the first chapter,' she said, smiling.

'You're right, it is. Now what do you say we get back on the horse and chase that sunset all the way home?'

'Which home?'

'It doesn't matter now, as long as we're both there.'

Other titles in the Linford Romance Library:

BORROWING ALEX

Cindy Procter-King

Nikki wants to get married more than anything. But what's she to do when her fiancé Royce is dragging his heels over setting a date? Why, fake a fling with the best man, of course! Ambushing Alex may be a tad desperate, but pretending she's hot for him just might kick-start Royce's attention . . . Alex is definitely not on board with this plan. But he quickly realizes Nikki isn't a wild party girl at all. She's cute, sweet — and faithful. Against his common sense, he's falling for her . . .

SEVEN LITTLE WORDS

Margaret Sutherland

Though romance writer Cathy Carruthers has been avoiding men in the wake of a painful break-up, when she meets literary novelist David Hillier neither can resist their powerful mutual desire. But her former partner is hunting her down, and her grandmother's illness means Cathy is landed with her tiny and courageous dog, Pixel. Meanwhile, David has his own problems: writer's block and the care of his father's retired guide dog. Pressures build on the couple, leading to conflict and friction — can they weather the storm together?

TRUE COLOURS

Wendy Kremer

When Kim inherits a seaside art gallery from her godfather, she unexpectedly decides to take it on — despite knowing next to nothing about art! Her new venture leads her to encounter the sophisticated art dealer, Mark, who proves both surprisingly helpful — and surprisingly desirable . . . But Kim is thrown off-kilter by the sudden appearance of a former boyfriend, and Mark is overshadowed by dark memories of his first wife. Will the pair succeed in conquering their trepidations, and finally reveal their true colours?

DANGEROUS LOVE

Teresa Ashby

Bram Fletcher, vet and lifeboat man, appears in Emergency Nurse Practitioner Regan Tyler's A&E department following his daring and reckless rescue of a little girl from a cliff during a raging storm. Despite the fact that she'd loved him once, Regan just wants him gone. But no matter what she does, their paths seem destined to cross, and his presence back in her life threatens to wreck everything . . .

MISTRESS OF MELLIN COVE

Rena George

When Dewi Luscombe is rescued from a shipwreck by the young Master of Mellin Hall, Kit St Neot, she finds she has lost her memory and doesn't know who she is. Touched by the girl's vulnerability and confusion, Kit decides to help her. But Dewi is haunted by the thought that someone close to her died in the shipwreck, and she sets off with Kit to ride across Cornwall to discover her true identity. Will Dewi ever regain her memory? And will Kit return her growing feelings for him?

H4413X

SWEET VENGEANCE

Roberta Grieve

Aspiring actress Kelley Robinson mistakes infatuation for love when she falls for charismatic media celebrity Carl Roche. Despite the warnings of her friends, she believes his promises and moves in with him. But when she discovers how he has deceived her, she is determined to get her revenge. Paul, a seemingly sympathetic journalist, offers to help put her plan into action. But is he only looking for a good story for his newspaper? Who can Kelley really trust?